KITTY ALONE: THREE FIRES

S. BARING-GOULD

ZINC READ

Published by
This edition copyright © 2024 by Zinc Read
Design and setting By Zinc Read
Email- zincread@gmail.com
ISBN-978-93-6243-261-2

CONTENTS

CHAPTER XIX
SUGGESTIONS OF EVIL

The crowd in the market-place and in the streets of Ashburton began to thin as the afternoon crept on. In vain did the showmen blow their trumpets, ring their bells, and invite to their entertainments. Those who had come to the fair had spent their loose cash. The proprietors of the stalls offered their wares at reduced prices, but found few purchasers. Young men who had been hired by the farmers swaggered about singing or shouting, some tipsy, others merely on the road to tipsiness. The ostlers in the inns were harnessing horses to the traps, market carts, gigs, dog-carts, that had brought in the farmers and their wives. Empty waggons were departing. The roads were full of streams of people flowing homeward to the surrounding villages.

Pasco Pepperill started with the schoolmaster. He had surrendered Kate to her father. The reins were in his hand, and he had whipped the cob, when he saw Coaker, the man from whom he had bought the wool, coming towards him.

The blood rushed into Pepperill's face.

"How d'ye do?" asked the farmer. "Going home?"

"I be," answered Pasco, with constrained anger.

"You'll find all the wool there. I sent off the lot this morning—three waggonloads."

"Why did you not inform me?—and I would have waited for it, and not come to the fair."

"I did not know how the weather might be—and I wished to be rid of it." Coaker laughed.

This angered Pasco further, and, losing command of himself, he said, "'Twas scurvy—that selling me at such a price when you knew wool was down."

"That was your concern. Each man for himself. But I reckon you've made a worse bargain at Brimpts, if, as they tell me, you have bought the wood."

"How so? Is not the timber first-rate?"

"Oh, the timber is good enough."

"Then what is wrong?"

"Have you been to Brimpts?"

"No—but Quarm has."

"Then you don't know the road. It is thus"—Coaker made a motion with his hand up and down. "The waves of the sea mountains high is nothing to it—and bad—the road is! Lor' bless y'! the cost o' moving the timber when cut will swallow up all the profits."

"Pshaw! The distance from Ashburton is only three miles."

"Better ten on a decent road. You'll never get the timber drawn, or, if you do, farewell to all profits. But when you have got it to Ashburton—who will buy it there?"

"Oh, Quarm has an idea of disposing of the oak to the Government—selling it to the dockyard at Devonport."

"How far off is that? Some five-and-twenty miles—and over the moor!" Coaker laughed.

"If I don't sell the oak, I am a"—Pasco's face was as red as blood. He checked himself from the confession that he would be a ruined man, and said between his teeth, "I'll never speak to Quarm again. He's led me into a pretty quandary."

"Quarm? He's a Jack-o'-lantern—don't trust he."

Coaker waved his hand, and, still laughing, went his way to the stable-yard to get his cob.

Pasco whipped his horse and drove homewards. His lips were closed, his brows knitted, he looked straight before him at the ears of his horse. He was in no disposition to speak. Nor, for the matter of that, was his companion. Bramber was thinking of Kitty, of the uncongenial surroundings, the hot-headed father, running himself and his brother-in-law into speculative ventures that must lead them to ruin; of the uncle, boastful, conceited, and withal stupid; of the hard, selfish aunt. He saw that young Pooke admired her, and this did not altogether please Bramber. Pooke might be well off and amiable, but he was dull of intellect—a boor—and could never be a suitable companion to the eager Kitty, whose mind was greedy for knowledge, and whose tastes were those of a class above that in which she was cast. The admiration of Jan Pooke brought on her contrariety. It had involved her in the quarrel between Jan and Noah, and had roused the jealousy of Rose Ash.

As the trap passed out of Ashburton, many a salutation was cast at Pepperill, but he hardly acknowledged any. He put up his hand and beat his hat down over his brows, then lashed savagely at his cob.

All at once something arrested his eye, and he instinctively drew up, then muttered, and whipped his brute again. What he had observed was a little plate, affixed to a house, with the title of the Insurance Company on it, with which he had that day had dealings.

"I wonder," thought Pasco, "what that house is insured for? Not for twelve hundred pounds, I'll swear."

Then a sense of bitterness rose in his heart against his brother-in-law for drawing him into this expense of insuring his property;—he had that day expended all the gold he had about him in paying the first premium. There remained only some silver in one pocket, and coppers in the other. Where was he to find the money for the payment of the oaks he had bought? Where that to meet the bill for the wool? The tanner would not pay enough for the bark to cover the cost of rending. Quarm had told him that the sap rose badly, and that it would involve much labour and waste of time to attempt to bark the trees.

Fevered with anxiety and disappointment, Pasco thrashed his cob savagely, and sent it along at its fullest pace, whirling past the gigs and waggons returning from the fair, and giving the drivers hardly time to get on one side to avoid him. He relieved his breast by swearing at them for their sluggishness in making way, and some retaliated with oaths, as, in order to escape him, they ran into the hedge or over a heap of stones.

Presently his horse slackened speed, as it reached a sharp ascent, and there Pasco met an empty waggon, with "Coaker—Dart-meet" on it. He stopped his panting horse, and shouted to the driver of the team, and asked whence he came.

"I've been to your place—Coombe Cellars," answered the waggoner. "Master sent me with a load of fleeces."

"Did my wife give you anything?"

"Not a glass of cider," answered the man. "We had to unload and do the work of hoisting into the warehouse ourselves—no one was about."

"She left it for me—she knew you would meet us."

Tossing his head, to shake off the depression that had come upon him, and with a flash of his vanity through the gloom, he put his hand in his pocket and drew out a couple of shillings.

"There," said he; "you'd have had more, but I have spent most of my cash at the fair. Buying, buying, buying, that's my trade. Go and drink a glass to my health."

Then he drove on.

On descending the hill another waggon was encountered. This was also one that had conveyed fleeces to Coombe Cellars. Pasco gave this driver a couple of shillings. Then he turned to Bramber and said, "Two years of wool—I paid as much as thirteen pence a pound, and I can't sell at tenpence. They say it is going down to sevenpence; that is nearly half what I gave. A loss to me of sixpence a pound; I have bought three waggonload. A good sheep may have sixteen pounds on his back, but the average is ten or eleven. Coaker must keep a couple of hundred. You're a schoolmaster; reckon that up—two hundred sheep at eleven. I'm not a quick man at figures myself."

"Nothing can be simpler than that calculation. Two thousand two hundred."

"Ah! But two years' wool?"

"Well, that is four thousand four hundred."

"And I have lost, say, sixpence a pound."

"Then you lose a hundred and ten pounds by the transaction."

"Think of that. A hundred and ten pounds—say a hundred and twenty. That is something for a man to lose and make no account of." The vanity of the man was flattered by the thought of the amount of his loss. "And then," said he, "there was what Coaker said about the oak. I've undertaken to lay out two hundred pounds on that; and there is the fellin' and cartin'—say another hundred. Suppose I lose this also—that is a matter of three hundred. With the wool, four hundred and twenty pound. I reckon, schoolmaster, you've never had the fingering of so much money as I am losing."

Bramber looked round at Pasco with surprise. He could not understand the sort of pride that was manifesting itself in the man.

"Are you able to meet such losses?"

"If not—I can but fail. It's something to fail for a good sum. But I'll not fail; I am full of resources." He beat the horse. "I shall sell the wool. It will go up. I shall sell the timber at a good figure, and pocket a thousand pounds. I am sorry I did not give those men half a crown each, but I have spent most of my money, and"—

Crash! He drove against a post, and upset the trap.

Pasco staggered to his feet.

"Schoolmaister—are you hurt?"

"No." Walter sprang to the horse and seized its head.

"It would have been best had I broken my neck and finished so," said Pepperill. Then he regretted the sudden outburst of despair, and added, "So some folks might ha' said, but I've disappointed 'em. I may have a chuck down, but I'm up again in a jiffy. That's been my way all along, and will be to the end."

One of the shafts was broken, and there ensued delay whilst it was being patched up with rope. Then, when they were able to pursue their career, Pasco was constrained to drive more carefully and less rapidly. Night was coming on as they neared Newton Abbot.

"I'll tell you what it is," said Pasco; "I'm uncommon hungry, and I'll just go into the first public-house and have a mouthful of something, and you shall do the same. The cob is a bit shaken with that spill, and I'll have the shaft fastened up firmer before we proceed. What say you? Here's the 'Crown and Anchor.' How the place is changed. Ah, ha! It is insured at the same office as I am. Why—bless my life!—the old inn was a ramshackle sort of a place."

Pepperill descended from his trap, and gave instructions to the ostler what he was to do to the broken shaft. "I'll pay you well if you do your work," said he. Then to Bramber, "Come in! Cold meat and bread-and-cheese, and a glass of ale. We need refreshment, and the house looks as if it could provide it. Don't be concerned about the cost. I don't suppose you are overflush with cash. I'll pay—you are my guest."

Pasco's self-conceit was a constant spring of energy in him. Dashed his spirits might be by disaster, but he speedily recovered his buoyancy, owing to this characteristic element in his nature. It is said that the fertility of Manitoba is due to the fact that below the surface the soil is frozen hard in winter, and during the summer the warmth of the sun penetrating ever farther thaws the ice, and thus water incessantly wells up, nourishing and moistening the roots of the corn. There was a perennial body of self-esteem deep in the heart of Pasco Pepperill, and this fed and sustained in vigorous growth a harvest of generosity in dealing with his inferiors, of liberality towards the poor, of display in his mercantile transactions, that imposed on the public and made it suppose that he was prosperous in his many affairs.

The landlord came to the door.

"How do you do, Mr. Pepperill?—glad to see you. You do not often favour me."

"Well—no. If I come this way I mostly stop at the Golden Sun. You see, you are rather near my home."

"I hope this, though the first visit, is not the last!"

"I daresay not. What brings me now is an accident. Can you let us have some supper?"

"Certainly. What would you like—cold beef, cold mutton, or chops and potatoes?"

"You have a supply of good things."

"I am obliged to have. I get plenty of custom now."

"What! more than of old?"

"Oh, double, since I have rebuilt my house."

"I see. The place is completely changed. You had but a poor sort of a tavern."

"Yes; and now"—the landlord looked round, smiled, and put his hands into his waistband—"middling good, I think."

"Uncommon," said Pasco. "I suppose it is the better look of the house that has brought better custom."

"That's just it. I had only common wayfarers before—mostly tramps. Now—the better sort altogether. Where I turned over a penny before, I turn over a shilling now."

"So you rebuilt your public-house to get better business?"

"Well, you see, I couldn't help myself. The old place caught fire and burnt down."

"And it did not ruin you?"

"Dear me, no. I was insured."

"So—that set you on your legs again?"

"It was the making of me, was that fire."

"How long had you been insured before you were burnt out?"

"Well, now, that is the curious part of the story," said the landlord; "hardly a week."

"And how did your place catch fire?"

"There was a tramp. I refused to take him in, as he had no money. That was the best stroke of business I ever did in my life. He hid himself in a sort o' lean-to there was over the pigs' houses, joined on to the house, and in it was straw. I reckon he went to sleep there with his pipe alight, and he set fire to the place."

"Was he burnt?"

"No; he got away all right; but the straw set fire to the rafters, and they ran into the wall. It was a poor old wall, with no mortar in it, and the rafters came in just under those of the upstairs chambers, so that when the roof of the linhay was afire, it set the house in a blaze too. That was how it all came about."

"And a good job it was for you!"

"It was the making of me."

Pasco was silent through the meal. He seemed hardly to taste what he was eating. He gulped down his food and drank copiously.

Bramber was relieved when he left. He was afraid Pepperill would drink more than he could bear. At the entrance to the village he left the cart, and thanked Pasco for the lift.

Pepperill drove on to Coombe Cellars.

As he came up, he saw his wife standing at the door with a light in her hand.

"Pasco, is that you?"

"Who else?"

"So, you are home at last. There has been the coal merchant here; he swears he will bring you no more, and that, unless you pay up this month, he will set the lawyers on you."

Pepperill flung himself from his cart.

"Heavens!" said he, looking sullenly at his stores; "if they would but burn!"

"Burn—what burn?" asked Mrs. Pepperill sharply. "Do you think you cannot leave the house for a day but some mischief must come on it? As if I were not to be trusted, and everything lay with you."

"I did not mean that, Zerah."

"Then what did you mean?"

"I meant that it might have got me out of difficulties."

"What might?"

Pasco did not answer.

"I should like to know how, if the store were to be burnt, any good would come of that. You've been drinking, Pasco."

"I'm insured," said he in a low tone.

"Oh, it has come to that, has it? Heaven help us!"

The woman beat her face with her open palms, turned, and went within.

CHAPTER XX
A FACE IN THE WATER

Kate Quarm was very happy on the moor. Her father had fetched her from Ashburton, and had lodged her in a cottage near Dart-meet, the point where the East and West Darts, rushing foaming from the moors, dancing over boulders, breaking over granite floors, plunging under tufts of golden gorse, and through brakes of osmund and male fern, reach each other and meet in one silver flood.

The weather was fine, though cold, that is to say, the sun was hot, but a keen east wind blew. But then this is one of the charms of the moor, that shelter can always be found from the wind. A mighty bank of mountains rose as a wall against the east, and in its dingles and dells, dense with gorse, now in blaze of flower, the air was warm, and balmy, and still.

At Coombe Cellars Kate had been kept continually employed; her aunt, an active woman, gave the child no rest. If she saw her flag in her work, Zerah goaded her with reproach to fresh activity; she was, moreover, never accorded a word of encouragement. Zerah accepted her work as a matter of course; if it was well done, that was but as it ought to be; everything that fell short of well, was occasion for a scolding. Kate's nature was one that needed repose from manual and sordid labour, for her mind desired to be active, and craved for freedom in which to expand, and for liberty to seek material on which to feed. This Zerah did not understand; with any other activity, except that of the body in scrubbing and rubbing, in cooking and baking, she had no sympathy; she entertained a positive aversion for books. She had no eye for beauty, no ear for melody, no heart for poetry.

Now Kate had leisure—now for the first time in her life in which her soul could draw its tender wings out of its case and flutter them in freedom. She felt much as must the May-fly when it breaks from its chrysalis.

It was, moreover, a joy to think that her father had considered her so far as to require her to be sent to the moor to recover. He usually paid little heed to Kitty, and now her heart was warm with gratitude because he had given her that very thing of all others which she most desired—rest in the presence of nature awakening under a spring sun.

Kate had another source of pleasure with her. As Walter Bramber parted from her at Ashburton, he put a little book into her hand, and said—

"I will lend it you. I know you will value it."

The book was Wordsworth's poems.

As she sat beside her father in the gig, she had her hand on the volume all the while, and her heart swelled with excitement and eagerness to read it. At night she hugged the book to her bosom, and fell asleep with both hands clasped over it. She could hardly endure that night should, with its darkness, deny her the happiness of reading. She woke early, and in the breaking daylight devoured the pages. As she read, she laughed and cried—laughed and cried with sheer delight. She had a book to read; and such a book!

This happy girl turned first to the verses on the daffodils that she had learned by heart, to make quite certain that she had all, that not a line had been missed, not a word got awry. Then she looked at the little poems on the celandine, and never did a famished child devour a meal with greater avidity than did Kate read and master these verses. There was much in Wordsworth that she could not understand, but the fact that she encountered passages that were unintelligible to her were of advantage, her clear intellect striking on these hard portions threw out sparks—ideas that had light in them. The book not only nourished her mind, but proved educative to her imagination.

Kate was at first overwhelmed with the flood of happiness that rolled over her. Her eyes could not satiate themselves with the beauty of the moorland scenery. She ran among the rocks, she dived into the coombs, she stepped on the boulders over the water, she watched the workmen engaged in felling trees.

Spring flowers peeped from behind rocks, bog plants peered out of the morasses. Kate began collecting. She dried the flowers between the leaves of her Prayer-book.

She scrambled among the towering rocks that overhung the Dart below the meeting of the waters, and watched the shadows and lights travel over the vast tract of moorland that stretched away as far as the eye could see in every direction but the east, where the river rolled out of its mountain cradle into a lap of the richest woodland. Sometimes the beauty of the scenery, the variety of landscape, were too much for her;

she sought change and repose by creeping among the rocks and drawing the book from her bosom.

Yet she could not read for long. The verses exacted close attention, and a flash of passing sun, or impatience at some passage she could not comprehend, made her close the volume and recommence her rambles. The exhilarating air, the brilliancy of the light, the complete change from the mild and languid atmosphere in the Teign estuary told on Kate's spirits and looks. Her cheeks gathered roundness and colour, and her tread acquired elasticity. Her spirits were light; they found vent occasionally in racing the cloud shadows over a smooth hillside.

One day, with her lap full of moss of every rainbow hue, she came upon the rector of Coombe-in-Teignhead, painting.

At her exclamation he turned, recognised her, and smiled.

"So—I thought I must soon see you," he said. "My dear little Kitty, I come with messages for you and kind inquiries."

"From whom—from uncle and aunt?"

"No; not from them. The schoolmaster, Mr. Bramber, when he heard whither I was coming, begged me to see you and ascertain how you were, and whether you liked the book he lent you."

"Oh, sir, I read it every day! I know several pieces by heart."

"That you are well, I see. I never saw you with such a glow of health and happiness in your bonnie face before."

"Thank you, sir. And will you see him soon?"

"Whom? Bramber?"

"Yes, sir," answered Kate, the glow in her face deepening. "And will you say that I have been picking the flowers as they come out, and I can find them, and that I do want to know what they are called? God brought the beasts to Adam to name them, and I do not think Adam can have been happy with the beasts till he had given each a name. It is so with me and the flowers. I see them, and I love them; but I don't feel content till I can tell what each is called. Mr. Bramber can name them all."

"You have made a collection?"

"Yes, I have dried them in my Prayer-book. They are waiting for Mr. Bramber to name. But"—Kate drew back—"I am in your way, sir; you are painting the old bridge."

"Yes; but you can sit down there if you like, and will not disturb me."

"May I? Oh, I shall be pleased."

Kate placed herself on a lichen-covered rock on one side, at a little distance from the water.

"I have left my few sheep for a couple of days," said Mr. Fielding apologetically, partly to Kate, mostly to himself; "but I do not think I have done wrong. Moses went up into the Mount, and came back to his people with his face shining. I do not know, but it seems to me that when I have been here aloft, speaking with nature and nature's God, face to face, that I can go back and carry with me some of the brightness and the freshness and the fragrance of the mountain. I may be wrong, finding an excuse for myself, because I love to come here."

"Please, sir," said Kate, "the Great Master of all dismissed the multitude and went up into the mountain apart."

"Yes, child, yes," answered the rector, painting as he talked; "and when He came down, He walked on the stormy waves. And I—His humble follower—I think I can tread on the troubles and cares of life erect, and not be swallowed up after I have been here."

"I do not know how I shall bear to go back to Coombe Cellars," said Kate sadly.

"You will go back braced to do your work. We cannot always play, Kitty dear. You know the fable of the bow. It was relaxed only that it might be the better weapon when restrung. Besides, when you return you will have pleasure."

"I shall think about my delightful holiday."

"Yes; and learn the names of the flowers you have dried in your Prayer-book," said Mr. Fielding, with a twinkle in the corner of his eye.

Kate dropped her head in confusion, but looked up again and said frankly, "Yes, that will be pleasant; and I can tell where each grew and how I found it."

"Tell whom—your aunt?" A faint crease in the old man's cheek showed he was smiling.

"No, sir! she won't care. I shall tell Mr. Bramber, if I have the chance."

"Kitty, I get very downhearted over my work sometimes. Then I come up here, and gather courage and strength, and—and trust, Kitty. You will return to Coombe Cellars strengthened and nerved to do your duty well and hopefully. Remember, it was kind of your aunt to let you come. She has to drudge hard whilst you are absent, but she does it because you have been ill and need relaxation in mind and invigoration of body. She does it, Kitty, because she *loves* you."

"Oh, sir!" Kate coloured with astonishment and with a twinge of pain at her heart.

"Yes, dear little friend, she loves you. She is not a demonstrative person. She is a clear-headed, practical woman. She has had a hard life, and much to try her, and to give her a cold and perhaps repellent manner. Nevertheless, her heart is sound and warm. When you were ill I spoke with her. I saw how anxious she was for your welfare. I saw into her heart, and I read love there."

Kate trembled, and let the mosses fall from her lap and strew themselves about her feet. The tears came into her eyes.

"Oh, sir, I should like to go home at once and do everything I can for her! I did not think she really cared for me."

"You do not return till your father decides that you are to go back to work. Then, you will return with a good courage, as I said."

"With all my heart!" answered Kate fervently, and her face brightened as though the sun shone on it.

Afraid of disturbing the old rector at his painting, Kate withdrew. She was happy at heart. What he had said had done her good. She had shrunk from the thought of return to the humdrum of her usual life, but Mr. Fielding had given her a motive for facing work with cheerfulness. It was a delight to her to think that her aunt loved her. She loved her aunt. Daily association with Zerah had made her cling to the hard, captious woman; she had had no one else to love, and the young heart must love someone.

Kate delighted to lie by the river, or lie on a rock in it, and look down into its pellucid pools, or at the flowing crystal where it broke between the stones. She was accustomed to the muddy estuary, and though the sea-water when it flowed was clear, it had none of the perfect transparency of this spring water near its source. The sea sweeping up the creek was as bottle-green glass, but this was liquid crystal itself, without colour of any sort, and through it everything in the depths was visible as though no medium intervened.

Kate could look at the shining pebbles, at the waving water-weed, at the darting fish. When she had left Mr. Fielding, she went to one of her favourite haunts beside the Dart, where it brawled over a cataract of rocks and then spread into a pool still as glass.

Now she saw what puzzled her, and set her active brain questioning the reason. As she looked into the water, she could see no reflection of her own face; the light sky was mirrored, and where the shadow of her head came, she could see far more distinctly to the bottom of the pool than elsewhere. Indeed, when a fish darted past she could discern its fins and scales, but when it passed beyond her shadow, its form became indistinct.

Then Kate rose on her elbows, and as she did this the sun caught her cheek and nose, and cheek and nose were at once reflected in the water, and where the reflection came, there the water was less transparent to her eyes.

To observe was to rouse in the girl's mind a desire to find an explanation for the very simple phenomenon that puzzled her.

She was thus engaged, raising her face, then a hand, so as to be now sunlit, then to intercept the light, and see what the effect was on the water, when she was startled to observe in the liquid mirror the reflection of a second face looking down from above. The sun was on it, in the eyes, and they glittered up at her from below.

With an exclamation of alarm, she turned and saw a man standing

CHAPTER XXI

AN OFFER

Kate rose to a sitting posture, and drew her feet under her, rested one hand on the rock, and with the other screened her eyes from the glare of the sun, to observe the intruder on her solitude.

Then she recognised Roger Redmore. He was without his coat, an axe over one shoulder. In his right hand he held a tuft of cotton grass dug up by the roots.

"I knowed as you wor here," said he, "but I dursn't speak before others, lest they should find me out who I wor."

"Are you living here, Roger?"

"I be working here at the felling Brimpts oaks. You see, your fayther, he's so little at Coombe that he don't know me, and I thought I might get money by working here. And I want you to do a little job for me."

"What is it, Roger?"

"There's two jobs. First, do y' see this here root o' white shiny grass? Well, I want y' to take it to Coombe and to set it on my little maid's grave. Stick the roots in. It may grow and it mayn't. Hereabouts it groweth mostly in wet land. But anyhows by it I shall know where the little maid lies when I come back to Coombe."

"You are returning, Roger?"

"Not by day. I reckon some night I shall be back just for an hour or so, and I want, when I does come, to go to the churchyard and find out at once where my darlin' lieth. If it be moonlight, or dimmets (twilight), and I see the little silver tuft glitter above her head, then I shall know where her be. I can't go wi' my wife; that would be tellin' folks I wor home agin. I mun go by myself. Whereabouts now have they put her?"

"By the wall where the cedar is, on the east side."

"There'll niver be no headstone there," observed Redmore, "but what o' that? When once I know where her lieth, sure but I'll put a fresh new tuft of silver tassels as oft as the old ones die, and I reckon they'll die, not being in a wet place. My little maid's grave won't be wet save wi' her father and mother's tears, and her faything he can't be there but on the sly, and now and then."

"I will do it for you gladly," said Kate. "When do you think you will be home?"

"Home!" repeated Roger; "I've no home—not like to have. My wife and my little ones, wherever they be, that's all the world to me, and I cannot see them but at night, and very chancy, when I don't think nobody's about. And t'other thing be this."

Roger put his hand into his pocket and drew forth some coin, and gave it to the girl.

"Take this to my old woman. I've earned wi' my work a bit o' money, and here is what I can send her. Tell her to leave the door ajar. I may come any night; but," he paused, "I reckon they've turned her out o' house and home now."

"Not yet, Roger," answered Kate. "Mr. Pooke has not insisted on her leaving at quarter-day, but I believe he has a fresh workman coming to him in a week, and then she will have to leave."

"And where will she go? Will they drive her into the street?"

"I really do not know; but"—she considered and said timidly, "I have had it on my heart, but have been afraid to speak of it as yet to my father. There is his cottage, never or hardly ever occupied. Now I will take courage, and beg him to let your wife go into it till something can be settled; but you must keep out of danger, and you are not safe here."

"I cannot go far till my wife and little ones are secure and have a home. Here no one know'th me, the other woodcutters are all men from the moor. There was but your father, and he did not recognise me when I axed him to take me on at felling the timber."

"I will entreat him to allow your wife and children to go into his house till something can be done for them. You will have to escape into another part of the country."

"Ay, I will go. If I were took, it would go bad with us all, and there'd be the shame on my little ones—that their father wor hanged. They'd never shake it off." Then he touched Kate on the head. "My hand be but a wicked un. It hev set fire to a rick, but it be the hand o' a hunted man, as be nigh crushed with sorrows, as was druv to wickedness thro' his sufferin's, and hev bitter repented it since, and swears he'll niver do it agin, so help me God!" He raised his hand solemnly to heaven. "That's one thing I ha' larned, as doin' wrong niver brings matters right. There wor just that gettin' drunk. Then there wor the cheek to Farmer Pooke. Then my heart were all wormwood; and when my little maid died, I thought it wor his doin'; and so in a way it wor, for I'd no work and no wage, and us was just about starvin', and I did that deed o' fire. It's kindled a fire in here"—he touched his heart—"that nothink can quench. The Lord ha' pity on me. I don't know as I'd ha' come to this mind but for you, little Kitty Alone, as was pitiful to me when I were bound and like to be given over to gaol, and you let me go, and fed me wi' crumbs out o' your hand; and now you will find a house for my dear ones." He laid his hand on her head again. "Mebbe the Lord'll hear a sinful thief o' a man, and I ax His blessin' on thee; an' if I can iver do anything to show you I'm thankful, I will. Amen."

"Hah!"

Roger. Redmore started. He was caught by a hand in his collar-band.

Kate sprang to her feet. Her uncle, Pasco Pepperill, was there. He had come up from behind unobserved, and had laid hold of the incendiary.

"I have you, you burning vagabond!" shouted he; "and by heaven! I'll hand you over to the constables, and see you hanged, as you deserve. Kate, run away—away at once!"

"Oh, uncle, do not be cruel! Let him go."

"You mind your business," answered Pasco sharply. "It's my belief you let him escape after Jan Pooke had bound him in the boat. Jan left you in charge, and Roger slipped away then."

"But think, uncle, of his poor wife and children."

With a sudden wrench Roger freed himself, and then, standing back with brandished axe, he said—

"Touch me, and I'll split your head."

"Get away from here," ordered Pasco, turning to his niece; "and as for you, Redmore, I want a word. You know very well that if I give the hue and cry you will be caught, even though now you have slipped from me. Lower your hatchet; I'm not going to hurt you if you be reasonable; but wait till that girl is out of earshot."

Pepperill put his hands into his pockets and watched Kate as she withdrew. Roger assumed an attitude of wariness. He was ready at a moment's notice to defend himself with his axe, or to take to flight.

"Look here," said Pasco, satisfied that he could not be overheard, "it seems to me that you, with your head almost in the noose, have done a wonderful silly thing to stay so near the scene of your crime."

"I'd my reasons as is not for you to know," answered Redmore surlily. "I'm sure you don't consarn yourself for me and mine so as to care."

"There you are mistaken," said Pasco. "I don't mean to say that I am deeply interested in you, but I don't intend, unless driven to it, to take any steps to get you acquainted with Jack Ketch."

"I can defend myself pretty well, suppose you do."

"I'm not the fool to risk my head in another man's quarrel."

"And I can take to my heels and find a hiding-place anywhere on these moors."

"Ay, and a starving-place where your bones will rot."

"What have you to say to me?"

Redmore spoke surlily. Now that his whereabouts was discovered, it would be needful for him to shift his place of refuge.

"I suppose you don't deny setting fire to Farmer Pooke's rick?" said Pasco.

Roger shrugged his shoulders and jerked his head.

"How did you do it? smoking a pipe under the tree when drunk?"

"No, it warn't."

"How was it, then?"

"I warn't drunk, niver but that once, and that wor just because o' Jackson's 'Tee-dum.' I've a bit of a orgin in zingin', and the innkeeper he wor terrible longing to have me in the choir. So he got me in, and they tried to teach me the tenor part o' Jackson's 'Tee-dum,' and I cu'dn't maister it noways; and they stood me liquor, and I tried, and I cu'd do naught wi' it. You see t'other parts went curling up and about, and bothered me. If they'd a' stopped and let me zing alone, I cu'd ha' done it. Then I went out into the open air, and it wor cold and frosty, and somehow I got mazed wi' the drink and the 'Tee-dum' together, and I rinned agin my maister, Farmer Pooke, and I reckon I zed what I ort not, and he turned me off. That wor it. I niver did it avor, and I'll niver do it agin. Save and presarve me from liquor and Jackson's 'Tee-dum'!"

"Never mind about that. So you didn't fire the rick with your pipe?"

"No, I didn't. If it had niver been for Jackson's 'Tee-dum,' I'd not now be in risk of bein' hanged."

"Of course it was Jackson did it all," sneered Pasco.

"I don't mean to say that. It wor the beginning on it. I were throwed out o' work, and were starvin', and my little maid, her died, and then I wor like a mazed chap, and I ran out wi' the cann'l, and so I did it."

"Oh, with the candle?"

"It wor a rushlight."

"I've heard of barns and storehouses being set fire to by men going into them to sleep, and lighting their pipes. There was the landlord of the Crown and Anchor at Newton. He had a miserable sort of a house, but a tramp got in one night"—

"What, into his house?"

"No, into a linhay over the pigstye, and slept there, or went there to sleep, and there was straw in the loft, and in smoking his pipe he managed to set fire to the straw, and then the whole public-house was in a blaze and burnt down."

"I've heard of that. Nobody knows what became o' the tramp. There wor roast pig found in the ashes, and whether roast tramp nobody cared to inquire."

"The inn has been rebuilt. They call it a hotel now."

"I daresay they does."

"The insurance money did that."

"I s'pose so. Lucky the house wor insured. I wish Varmer Pooke 'ad been."

"You do?"

"I reckon I does. I'm sorry for what I did when I wor in a b'ilin' blue rage. Now I can't get over it noways, and you may tell'n so."

"Why, that fire was the making of the landlord. He feels no ill-will against the tramp. What are you going to do with yourself now?"

"I don't know."

"I suppose you will want to see your wife again?"

"I s'pose I shall."

"For that you will return to Coombe?"

"In coorse I must."

"At night—lest you should be seen?"

"Ay—to be sure."

"You will lurk about—be in hiding. I'll tell you what, I'm your good friend. I will do you no harm. I'll just leave the door of my stores open—unhasped; and if you want to creep in, there's a lot of wool and other things there, you can be warm there, Roger, warm in the wool."

"Thanky', sir. You'll not peach?"

"And if—if you like a pipe—well"—

"No, Mr. Pepperill, I won't do you that ill turn if you're so good to me—and the little maid, Kitty, too."

"Oh, I did not mean that. I can't say but if a spark chanced to fall among the wool, and the whole was to blaze away, I should be sorry. I can't say that I should be troubled, any more than was the landlord at Newton when the tramp set fire to his linhay over the pigs."

Redmore said nothing. Pepperill spoke slowly, and did not look the man in the face as he spoke.

"If that chance was to happen to me as happened to the man at Newton, it might, there's no saying, be a saving of me from a great misfortune, and—I shouldn't mind being a liberal friend, and helping you out of the country."

"That is what you mean, is it?"

"It might be a convenience to both of us."

"'Tis a wonderful world," exclaimed Redmore, "when the biggest rascals go free, and one of them be you! A little rascal like me, who's sorry that ever he done wrong, is chivied like a mad dog."

"Well—what do you say?"

"You're a rascal and I despise you," cried Roger, and turned to go.

"Will you have me as your friend or your enemy?"

"Your enemy rather than friend on them terms."

"Then I'll hang you!" exclaimed Pasco, and set off running in the direction of Brimpts.

CHAPTER XXII
A RACE FOR LIFE

Kate had walked away without a thought of attempting to gather the subject of her uncle's conversation with Redmore. She resolved at once to seek her father and obtain from him permission to house the unfortunate wife with her children in his cottage. She had been told that he had gone to a farm lying somewhat to the right of the Ashburton road, near the prominent and stately rock citadel of Sharpitor. She therefore ascended the long, steep hill, up which scrambles the high road from Dart-meet.

Halfway up the ascent is an oblong mass of granite, lying in the moor, which goes by the name of the Coffin Stone, because on it coffins are rested by those who are bearing a corpse to its lasting resting-place in the distant churchyards of Buckland or Ashburton. Kate had reached this stone, and was panting for breath, when she heard shouts and cries in the valley she was leaving, and, leaping upon the Coffin Stone, she saw a swarm of men on the opposite bank of the Dart—the Brimpts side—running in the direction of the bridge, headed by her uncle, who was then levelling a gun he carried.

From her elevation she could not only see but hear everything.

"An incendiary! He set fire to a stack. A pound to any man who takes him, alive or dead!" shouted Pasco, and to Kate every word was audible. Then she saw the flash of the gun, and a little later heard the report. The shot had missed, for her uncle urged on the men to run and not let the scoundrel escape, and he himself lagged behind to reload his barrel.

She looked for the fugitive, but was able to see him for one moment only, as he leaped a ruinous fence in his flight down stream.

Why was he taking that direction? Because the way into the fastnesses of the moorland was closed to him by his pursuers. He could not run up the hill that Kate ascended, as he would be exposed throughout, without the smallest cover, to the gun of Pepperill. Though a course down the river led ultimately into inhabited land, yet between the moor and population lay the great woodland belt of Buckland and Holme Chase, where the river wound its way in sweeps among dense forest and rock, and where Redmore knew he could hide with the greatest ease. But before he could be in the woodland he had a long stretch of moor to traverse, where there was no road, at best a fisherman's track, among rocks scattered in confusion, among heather and furze bushes, with here and there sloe and thorn trees and an occasional "witch beam" or rowan growing out of the rocks. Almost immediately after the junction of the East with the West Dart, the united stream doubles round Sharpitor, that shoots high above it on one side, and under the ridges of Benjietor on the other side, in whose lap grows a little copse, and which, from its crags to the water's edge, is green with bracken in summer, but at this period was russet with withered leaves. Thence smoke rose—some boys had ignited the gorse, and the flames ran among the withered ferns and the fallen oak-leaves, and blackened and burnt the copse.

Kate hastened on her way. She knew that on reaching the head of the ridge a short distance intervened between the road and the precipices of Sharpitor that overhung the ravine. Thence she could see all that followed—if Roger Redmore succeeded in turning the moorland spur round which the river foamed.

Hot, trembling, and breathless, Kate ran, then halted to gasp, then ran on, and did not rest for more than a minute till she had reached the vantage-point on the rocks, and looked down into a wondrous ravine of river, granite boulder, and glaring golden furze, and with the blue smoke of the smouldering fern forming a haze that hung in its depths, but which rose in places above the rocky crests of the moor and showed brown against the luminous sky.

Kate ensconced herself among the piles of granite, with a "clatter," as it is locally termed, at her feet, a mass of rocky ruin, composed of granite, in fragments of every size and in various conditions of disintegration.

She saw Redmore as he doubled the foot of the mountain, and for awhile had the advantage of being invisible to his pursuers, and safe from the gun of Pepperill. He stood on a great rock half-way out of the water, and looked about him. He was resolving what to do, whether to continue his course down stream, or to endeavour to conceal himself at once. The fire and smoke on the farther side in the bosom of Benjietor made it impossible for him to secrete himself there—every lurking-place was scorched or menaced by the flames. The slope of Sharpitor on his left, though strewn with the wreckage of the crags above, offered no safe refuge; it was exposed to full light, without any bushes in it other than the whortle and heather. Roger did not take long to make up his mind; he pursued his course down the river, now wading, then scrambling over stones, then leaping from rock to rock, and then again flying over a tract of smooth turf. Occasionally the wind, playing with the smoke, carried a curl of it across the river, and drew it out and shook it as a veil, obscuring Redmore from the eyes of Kate, who watched him in panting unrest, and with prayers for his safety welling up in her heart. Then shouts—the men who hunted him had rounded the flank of Shapitor, and had caught sight of the man they were endeavouring to catch. One fellow, with very long legs, familiar with the ground, accustomed all his life to the moor, was making great way, and bade fair to catch Roger.

Redmore looked behind him. He had cast away his axe, and was therefore unarmed, but was lightened for the race.

"A sovereign to the man who catches him!" yelled Pepperill. "Knock him down, brain him!"

Then one man heaved a stone, picked out of the river, and threw it. A vain attempt. He was not within reach of Redmore; but in a pursuit, none can quite consider what is possible, and measure distances with nicety, without much greater coolness than is possessed by men running and leaping over difficult ground. The long-legged man kept forging ahead, with his elbows close to his sides; he had distanced the rest. He was fleet of foot, he sprang from stone to stone without pausing to consider, and without ever missing his footing. Roger advanced slowly: he was unaccustomed to such difficult ground; sometimes he fell; he floundered into the river up to his armpits and scrambled out with difficulty. His pursuer never got into the water. The man had not merely long legs, he had a long nose and protruding eyes, and as he ran, with his elbows back, he held his forefingers extended, the rest folded. Every stride brought him nearer to Redmore, and Roger, who had just scrambled upon a rock in the river, saw that he must be overtaken, and he prepared for the inevitable struggle.

Kate, leaning forward in her eagerness, at this moment displaced a large block, that slid down, turned on its edge and rolled, then leaped, then bounded high into the air, crashed down on another rock, and from it leaped again in its headlong course.

The girl held her breath. It seemed as though the rock must strike the running pursuer, and if it struck him it would inevitably be his death. The rattle of displaced stones, the crash of the block as it struck, the cries of those behind, who saw the danger, arrested the long-legged man. He halted, and looked up and around, and at that moment the stone whizzed past and plunged into the river. Kate saw in a moment the advantage thus gained, and in palpitating haste threw down every stone she could reach or tilt over from its resting-place, where nicely balanced, thus sending a succession of volleys of leaping, whistling stones across the path, between the pursued and the pursuers.

She heard shouts and execrations from those who were coming up, and who stood still, not daring to continue their course, and run the risk of having their brains beaten out by one of the falling stones. She regarded them not. Her one idea was to save Roger. She could see that the man for whom she acted had recognised her intervention, and continued his flight. She could see that the pursuers were stationary, uncertain what to do.

Then her uncle again raised his gun. Kate put her hands to her mouth and called to Roger, who looked over his shoulder, and dropped behind a stone just as the gun was discharged.

Then he picked himself up once more and ran on. Kate dared not desist. She continued to send block after block rolling. Some were shattered in their descent, and resolved themselves into a cloud of whizzing projectiles. Some in striking the soil set a mass of rubble in motion that shot down and threw up a cloud of dust.

She was hot, weary, her hands wounded. But the consciousness of success strung her to renewed exertion. Pasco Pepperill called the party in pursuit together. He shouted up the height to the girl. Who it was there engaged in dislodging stones he couldn't discern, for Kate kept herself concealed as far as possible, and the confusion of the granite rocks thrown into heaps and dislocated, served to disguise the presence of anyone among them. He threatened, but threatened in vain; Kate did not stay her hand to give time to listen to what he cried.

After a brief consultation, as the avalanche did not decrease, the party resolved to cross the river and continue the pursuit down it on the farther side, through the smoke and over the ashes of the conflagration. By this means Roger Redmore could be kept in sight, and possibly it would be more easy to run over the charred soil among bushes reduced to ash. Moreover, few, if any, of the stones dislodged by Kate had sufficient weight and velocity to carry them to the farther side of the river.

Accordingly, the party began to step on the rocks that projected from the water, or to wade, so as to reach the farther side, Pepperill lingering behind reloading his gun, and keeping his eye on the fugitive. Then a sudden idea struck him, and, calling to the men to proceed as they had proposed, he started to climb the steep tide of Sharpitor, at a point where not menaced by the falling stones, judging that by this means he would dislodge the person who had come to the assistance of the fugitive, and at the same time be able to follow the flight of the latter with his eye better than below, and to obtain a more leisurely shot at him when a suitable occasion offered, as his poising himself on a rock, or halting to resolve on his course.

Kate desisted from sending down volleys of stones, till the occasion should arise again. She watched the flight of Roger, and perceived that he was aiming at a coppice which was in a fold of the hills undiscernible by those on the farther side of the river; by means of this coppice, if he could reach it, Roger would be able to effect his escape.

In three minutes he was safe; then Kate drew a long breath. At the same moment she was touched on the shoulder, and, looking round, saw her father.

"What's all this about? What's this shouting and firing of guns?"

"Oh, father, I hope I have not done wrong! Uncle and all the men are after Roger Redmore."

"Who is he?"

"The man who burnt Mr. Pooke's ricks, and he has been working for you here—and uncle recognised him, and sent the men to take him, and he ran away, and I have helped him."

"You?"

"Yes; by rolling down rocks."

Jason burst into a fit of laughter. "Come, that is fine. You and I, Kitty, aiders and abettors of an incendiary. Is he clear off now?"

"Yes; but here comes uncle up the steep side."

Jason hobbled to the edge of the rock, and, leaning over called, "Halloo, Pasco! Here we are waiting for you—Kitty Alone and I."

CHAPTER XXIII

BORROWING

"It is you—you two!" exclaimed Pepperill, as he reached the summit. He gasped the words; he could not shout, so short of breath was he. His face with heat was purple as a blackberry. "What's the meaning of this?" He held to a projection of granite, and panted. "Interfering with law—protecting a scoundrel." He paused to wipe his face. "A malefactor—a criminal—guilty"—again gasped like a fish out of water—"guilty of incendiarism, of arson, of felony!"

"Why, Pasco, you're hot. Keep cool, old boy," said Jason, laughing. "Who has created you constable, or sheriff of the county, that you are so anxious to apprehend rogues?"

"Rogues? rogues? Only rogues assist rogues in escaping the reward of their deeds."

"Is there a warrant out for his apprehension?"

"I don't know."

"Then what on earth makes you put yourself in a heat and commotion to catch him?"

Pasco mopped his brow, and, tearing up some ferns, dry though they were, proceeded to fan his face.

"Why? Do you ask? For the public security, of course. And now"—again he puffed—"now I can't talk; my wind is gone."

Pepperill looked into the ravine. He could see that the men on the farther side of the stream were at a nonplus. The fugitive had escaped them, had dived out of their sight into the coppice-wood, and they knew that pursuit was in vain. He turned sharply on his brother-in-law.

"This is your doing—you and Kate. First you give him work, and then you let him escape. He who helps a felon is a felon himself."

"My dear Pasco," said Jason Quarm, laughing, "what makes you so fiery in this matter?"

"Fiery? of course I'm fiery. And look there, Jason! There are the workmen, a dozen of them, doing nothing, and we shall have to pay their wages for a half day, and nothing to show for it."

"Whose fault is that? You sent them from their tasks."

"Yes, to catch a villain."

"Which was no concern of yours."

"It is a concern of mine, and of every honest man. How can one be safe with such a malefactor at large? I have my house, my stores; I shall not be able to sleep at night with ease, knowing that this fellow is at large. If anything happens, I shall come on you."

"You'll get nothing from me."

"That is the worst; I know it. Why did you help the man to escape? No one is safe—no one. And I, least of all; for now he regards me as his enemy. He has sworn vengeance; he may come on me and cut my throat."

"Not much throat to be cut, Pasco."

"There is my money-box"—

"Box, not money."

"He may set fire to my house—my barns—burn me and my wife—your sister—Kitty—your daughter. Don't you care for that?"

"I am not afraid. If you went after him, and have angered him, well, we helped him, as you suppose, and have won his good-will."

"As I know. Have I not found you here? Who else could have rolled down the rocks? Show me your hands. There, I said so!—there is blood on Kate's hands; they are cut and bruised. She has been doing what she could; and you, her father, who ought to have known better, have encouraged her. Rascals! rogues!—rogues all!"

"And oh, how honest am I!—eh, Pasco?"

"Of course I'm an honest man. I don't encourage burglars, and murderers, and incendiaries."

"I did not know that Redmore was a murderer or a burglar."

"Who can say but, having been an incendiary, he may go on to murder and plunder; these things run together. One who can commit arson is capable of doing the other crimes as well. I shall have to drive back to Ashburton alone."

"Kitty returns with you."

"What help is there in Kitty? That fellow Roger, full of rage and desire of revenge, is about the woods, and may shoot me."

"He has not a gun."

"He may spring upon me with his axe."

"He has thrown it away," said Kate.

"You mind your own concerns," exclaimed the angry man, turning on his niece. "There are plenty of ways in which he may fall on me and murder me, and then he will pick my pockets and make off in my clothes, and Kitty will help him."

"You are talking nonsense, Pasco. Are you such a weakling that you cannot defend yourself? But, pshaw! the man will not injure you."

"He will steal by night to Coombe. His wife is there; his children are there. He knows where I am. He has sworn revenge against me."

"When? When he escaped?"

"No; before I set the men after him."

"Before he knew you would hunt him? A probable story!"

"Probable or improbable, it is true. I threatened him, and I would have arrested him, but could not. Kate knows I had him by the throat; but he was armed with his axe, and I could not retain him. Then he swore he would do me an evil turn, and he will keep his word."

"He cannot harm you; he is afraid for himself."

"He can harm me. He can do to my house, my stores, what he did to Pooke's rick."

"Well, that would not hurt you greatly; you are insured over value."

"Not over value, with the wool in."

"You were a fool about that wool, Pasco. Why did you not consult me before dealing with Coaker? I knew of the fall."

"Oh, you know everything. You knew that the Brimpts oak bark was worth three times more than it is; and now you are felling, without considering that the bark at present is practically worthless."

"The sap doesn't run."

"If the sap ran like the Dart, it would not make the bark sell for tan. You either knew nothing about the conditions, or you wilfully deceived me; and I dare be sworn it was the latter. I can believe even that of you now, a favourer of incendiaries."

"Come, do not be extravagant. What other criminals have I ever favoured?"

"I am too hot and too angry to argue," retorted Pasco. "But I want to know something for certain about this Brimpts wood. It is well enough to cut it down, but what I want to know is, how will you transport the oak so as to make it pay?"

"Sell on the spot."

"To whom?"

"To timber merchants."

"They will reckon the cost of carriage."

"We shan't have to pay for it."

"We shall sell at a good price."

"We shall sell! Such oak as Brimpts oak is not to be had every day."

"Have you offered it to anyone—advertised it?"

"No, I have not. Time for that when it is all felled."

"You will make as much a misreckoning in this as you have along of the bark."

"Trust me. The oak will sell high."

"You said the same of the bark. All your ducks are swans. I *must* have money."

"So must I," said Quarm. "I want it as the March fields want April showers."

"I am in immediate need," urged Pepperill.

"In a fortnight I shall require money to pay the men their wages," observed Quarm.

"I have nothing. You were right; I have a cash-box, but no cash in it. I have paid away all I had."

"Dispose of something," said Quarm cheerily.

"Dispose of what? Coals? No one wants coals now."

"Then something else."

"Wool, and lose on every pound? That were fatal. I have not paid for all the wool yet. I want money to satisfy the coal-merchant, money to meet the bill I gave Coaker; and then the agent for the bank which has its hold on the Brimpts estate says we may not remove a stick till everything is paid."

"Then do not remove," said Quarm. "Sell on the spot."

"To whom?"

"There are plenty will buy."

"Why have you not advertised?" asked Pasco testily.

"For one thing, because I did not know you were in immediate need of cash; for the other, because, till the timber is down, it cannot be measured. Never sell sticks standing. A timber merchant will always buy the trees before felled, and many a landowner is fool enough to sell standing trees. The merchant knows his gain; the landlord does not know his loss."

"Felled or unfelled, I must realise. My condition is desperate. I cannot meet any of the demands on me."

Pepperill had lost his purple colour. He wiped his brow again, but this time the drops did not rise from heat, but from uneasiness of mind.

"You have drawn me into this Brimpts venture, and I have now all my fortunes on one bottom. If this fails, I am ruined; there will remain nothing for me but to sell Coombe Cellars, and then—I am cast forth as a beggar into the roads. I have trusted you; you must not fail me."

"Oh, all will come right in the end."

"The end—the end! It must come right now. I tell you that I have to meet the demands of the bank, or I can do nothing with the sale of the oak, and all now hangs on that. Owing to the ruinous purchase of Coaker's fleeces, I am driven to desperate straits. I cannot sell them at a loss. I calculated it with the schoolmaster—a loss of some hundred and twenty pounds. You must help me out of my difficulty."

"I can but suggest one thing. Go to Devonport, and see if the Government Dockyard will buy the oak. Ship-building can't go on without material. If Government will take the timber, you need not concern yourself about the bank's demand; it will be satisfied, and more than satisfied, that the money is safe. Bless you! in these times a man is happy to see his money within twelve months of him, and know he must have it."

"I don't mind; but I'll go to Devonport at once," said Pepperill.

Whilst the conversation thus detailed was taking place, the three had crossed a strip of moor that intervened between Sharpitor and the high road, walking slowly, for Pasco was fagged with his scramble, and Jason was crippled.

"I don't mind," said Pasco again. "But I shall want a few pounds to take me there, and my pockets are empty."

"I can't help you. Mine wouldn't yield if wrung out."

"Here comes the parson," said Pepperill—"our parson, jogging along as if nothing were the matter and went contrary in the world. I'll borrow of him."

"Oh, uncle," protested Kate, flushing crimson, "pray do not, if you have no chance of paying."

"You impudent hussy, mind your own concerns," answered Pasco angrily. "I, with no chance of paying! I'm a man of means. I'll let you see what that signifies. How d' y' do, parson?"

"What! my churchwarden?" exclaimed Mr. Fielding, drawing rein. "What brings you to the moors?"

"Business, sir, a trifle with regard to oak timber. I've bought the Brimpts wood—cost me a few hundred, and will bring me a thousand."

"Glad to hear it, Mr. Pepperill;—and then we shall have a double subscription to our school."

"I daresay, Mr. Fielding; I'm a free man with my money, as you and others have found. And, by the way, talking of that, could you kindly accommodate me with a little loan of a few pounds. I started from home without a thought but of returning to-day, and I learn that the Government has an eye on these oaks—first-rate timber—and I must to

Devonport to strike a bargain. I won't come to their terms, they must come to mine. Such timber as this is worth its weight in gold."

"How much do you want, Mr. Pepperill?"

"How much can you spare, Mr. Fielding?"

"Well, let me see." The rector of Coombe opened his purse. "I have about six guineas here. I shall want to retain one for current expenses. When can you let me have the loan returned."

"Any day. I'll drop you a line to my wife—or—on my return. I'm only going to Devonport to get the best price for the timber, and then I shall be back. If you can spare me five guineas—or five sovereigns—I shall be obliged. You know me—a man of substance, a man of means, a warm man. We represent the Church, do we not, Mr. Fielding? and hang Dissenters all, say I."

"I can let you have five pounds," said the rector; "I see I am short of silver."

"That will suffice," answered Pasco, with dignity. "I will let you have it back directly I have settled with Government about the oaks."

Mr. Fielding gave Pepperill the gold, then excused himself, as he desired to reach home before dark, and rode on his way.

"I had no idea that to borrow was so easy," said Pasco. "Of course, all depends on the man who asks. Everyone knows me—sound as the Bank of England."

"And same thing," said Quarm; "all depends on the man solicited."

Then Pepperill, with his hands in his pockets and head in the air, his spirits revived as though he had borrowed five hundred pounds in place of five pounds, walked towards Dart-meet Bridge humming the old harvest song,—

"We've cheated the parson; we'll cheat him again;
For why should the vicar have one in ten?
One in ten?
We'll drink off our liquor while we can stand,
And hey for the honour of Old England!
Old England!"

CHAPTER XXIV

SHAVINGS

With five pounds in his pocket, Pepperill drove to Plymouth and on to Devonport. His moral courage was up again now he had gold to spend. When his purse was empty, his spirits, his tone of mind, became depressed and despairing. A very little—a few pounds—sufficed to send them up to bragging point. There was no limit to his self-complacency and assurance as he appeared at the dockyard.

His spirits, his consequence that had so risen, were doomed to sink when he learned that no oak, however good, was required. Okehampton Park, the finest, the most extensive in the county, had been delivered over by the impecunious owners to the woodman; thousands of magnificent trees, as ancient and as sound as those of Brimpts, had been felled. The market was glutted, oak of the best quality sold cheap as beech; and the Government had bought as much at Okehampton as would be needed for several years.

"That is the way with all Government concerns, stupidly managed by blunderheads. I can do business better with private firms. I know very well what this means—to grease the palms of the authorities. I am a man of principle—I won't do it." So said Pepperill, as he swung away from the dockyard. "Bah! I've always been a staunch supporter of Church and State, churchwarden and Tory. If the Government can't oblige me when I want a little favour done, but must go to the cheapest shop, blow me if I don't turn Whig—that's not bad enough—roaring Radical, and cry, Down with the Constitution and the Crown! As for the Church, I don't say as I'll go in for disestablishment and disendowment just now. There is some benefit in an Established Church when it will accommodate one at a pinch with five pounds, and don't press to have it returned till convenient."

Pasco betook himself now to private firms of shipbuilders, but was unable to dispose of his timber. The mowing down of Okehampton Park had flooded the market with first-quality oak. One firm was inclined to deal with him, if he would draw the timber into Plymouth. Sanguine at his undertaking, he returned to Dart-meet to drive a bargain with some of the farmers on the moor for conveying the oak logs to the seaport town. He found that their charges were likely to be high. The way was long, the road hilly, in places bad. It would take them two days at least to convey each load, with a pair of horses, or a team of three, to Plymouth; and what was one load?—what, but a single log. Then there was the return journey, that might be done in a long day; but after three such days, the horses would not be fit for work on the fourth. A pair of horses was ten shillings; and for three days—that was five-and-twenty; but in reality three horses would be needed, and that would be thrice fifteen—two pounds five for each stick of timber before it was sold. As for the spray,—all the upper portion of the trees,—that would have to be disposed of on the spot; and Pepperill foresaw, with something like dismay, that he would get no price for it. The expense of carriage would deter all save moor farmers from purchasing, and they were so few in number, that the supply would exceed the demand, especially as they could have as much turf as they wanted for the cutting; and practically not sufficient would be got from the sale of the faggot wood to pay for the felling of the timber.

It is one of the peculiar features of England that our roads are absolutely without any of the facilities which modern engineering would yield to travellers on wheels. Our ancient highways were those struck out by packmen, and when wheeled conveyances came into use, the carriages had to scramble over roads only suitable for pack-horses. In France and Germany it is otherwise, there modern road-engineering has made locomotion easy. The main arteries of traffic ascend and descend by gentle gradients, and make sweeps where a direct course would be arduous and exhaustive of time.

Now the road from Dart-meet, a main thoroughfare over the moor, might be carried along the river-bank, with a gentle fall of a hundred feet in the mile, for six miles. But instead of that, it scrambles for a mile up a hogsback of moor, nearly five hundred feet in sheer ascent, then comes down to the Dart again; then scrambles another ridge, and then again descends to the same river. Nothing could be easier than to have a trotting road the whole way; but in mediæval times packmen went up and down hill; consequently we in our brakes, and landaus, and dog-carts must do the same; not only so, but the transport of granite, peat, wool, and the oaks from the felled forest was rendered a matter of heavy labour and great cost. Pepperill saw that it was quite hopeless to expect to effect any dealings on the Ashburton side, on account of the tremendous hills that intervened.

With rage and mortification at his heart, he sought for his brother-in-law, and could not find him. He was told that Quarm had gone to

Widdecomb. Some repairs were to be done in the church, the parsonage was to be rebuilt, and he was going to ascertain whether oak timber would be required there, and how much, and whether he could dispose of some of the wood of Brimpts for this object.

He could not wait for Quarm. He wanted to be home. He was to convey Kate to Coombe Cellars—it had been so arranged. His wife was impatient for her return, had begun to discover what a useful person in the house Kate was. Moreover, the moor air had done what was required of it, had restored health to the girl's cheeks.

In rough and testy tone, Pepperill told his niece to put together her traps and to jump up beside him.

"You've had play enough at our expense," he growled. "Your aunt has had to hire a girl, and she's done nothing but break, break—and she's given Zerah cheek—awful. Time you was back. We can't be ruined just because your father wants you to be a lady, and idle. We're not millionaires, that we can afford to put our hands in our pockets and spend the day loafing. If your father thinks of bringing you up to that, it's a pity he hasn't made better ventures with his money." After a pause, with a burst of rancour, "His money! *His* money, indeed! it is mine he plays games with, it is my hard-earned coin he plays ducks and drakes with—chucks it away as though I hadn't slaved to earn every groat."

As he talked, he worked himself up into great wrath; and like a coward poured forth his spite upon the harmless child at his side, because harmless, unable to retaliate. He was accustomed to hear his wife find fault with Kate, and now he followed suit. We all, unless naturally generous, cast blame on those who are beneath us; on our children, our servants, the poor and weak, when we are conscious of wrong within ourselves, but are too proud for self-accusation. It has been so since Adam blamed Eve for his fall, and Eve threw the blame on the serpent.

"I don't hold with holiday-making," said Pasco. "It is all very well for wealthy people, but not for those who are workers for their daily bread. I might ha' been, and I would ha' been, an independent man, and a gentleman living on my own means, but for your father. He's been the mischief-maker. He has led me on to speculate in ventures that were rotten from root to branch, and all my poor savings, and all that your aunt Zerah has earned by years of toil—it is all going—it is all gone. There are those workmen cutting down the oak, they are eating my silver, gorging themselves on my store, and reducing me and Zerah to beggary. To the workhouse—that's our goal. To the workhouse—that is where your father is driving us. What are you staring about you for like an owl in daylight?"

"Oh, uncle," answered Kate in a voice choked with tears, "I have been so happy on the moor, and it is all so beautiful, so beautiful—a heaven on earth; and I was only looking my last—and saying good-bye to it all."

"Not listening to what I said?"

"Indeed I was, and I was unhappy—and what you said made me feel I should never come back here, and I must work hard now for Aunt Zerah. There was no harm in my looking my last at what I have loved and shall not see again! It is so beautiful."

"Beautiful? Gah!" retorted Pasco. "A beastly place. What is beautiful here? The rocks? The peat? The heather? Gah! It is all foul stuff—I hate it. What are you hugging there as if it were a purse of gold?"

"Oh, uncle, it is something I love so! The schoolmaster sent it me by Mr. Fielding. It's only a book."

"A book? of what sort? Let me see."

Kate reluctantly produced the cherished volume.

"Pshaw!" said Pasco, rejecting it with disgust. "Poetry—rotten rubbish—I hate it. It's no good to anyone, it stuffs heads with foolery. I wish I was king, and I'd make it a hanging matter to write a line of poetry and publish it. It's just so much poison. No wonder you don't like work, when you read that vile, unwholesome trash."

Kate hastily folded up the volume and replaced it in her bosom.

"No wonder you and your father encourage vagabonds and incendiaries if you read poetry."

"Father did not help Roger Redmore to escape," said Kate. "It was I who rolled down the stones. Father came up when he had already got away to a hiding-place. I, and I alone, did it."

"More shame to you! You're a bad girl, a vicious girl, and will come to no good."

He continued grumbling and snarling and harping on his grievances, and, for some while, jerking out spiteful remarks. Presently he relapsed into silence, and let the tired cob jog along till he reached a point where, near Holne, roads branched: one went down the hill to Ashburton without passing through the village, the other went round by the church and village inn. Here Pasco drew up, uncertain which road to take. There was not much difference in the distance. The direct way was the shorter, but by not more than half a mile, whereas the other afforded opportunity for refreshment.

At this point was a carpenter's shop. The workman was not there, but he had left his shop open, and outside was a great pile of shavings.

As Pasco sat ruminating, doubtful which way to take, his eye rested for some while on the shavings. Presently, without a word, he got out of the conveyance, let down the back of the cart, collected as many shavings as he could carry, and thrust them in, under the seat. He went back to the pile, took as many more as he thought would suffice, and crammed the body of the cart with them. Then, still without speaking, he shut the back, remounted, and drove down the shortest way—the steep hill, the direct road to Ashburton that avoided the village.

"Uncle!" said Kate, after a while.

Pepperill started, as though he had been stung. "Bless me!" he exclaimed; "I had forgotten you were here."

"Uncle," pursued the girl, "you know my dear mother left a little money, a few hundred pounds, for me. And my father is trustee, and he has charge of it, and has invested it somewhere for me. If you are in difficulties, and really want money, I am sure you are heartily welcome to mine. I will ask my father to let you have the use of it. I cannot do other—you and Aunt Zerah have been very kind to me."

"Yes, that we have, and been to tremendous expense over your keep; and there was your education with Mr. Puddicombe, and the doctor's bill coming in, and the medicines; and there has been your clothing—and you have always eaten—awful. That costs money, and ruins one. Yes, you are right, you couldn't do other. I had not thought of that. But I don't know what your father will say."

"In a very few years I shall be old enough to have it as my own to do with as I like. I do not think that my father will object to its being employed as I wish. And I know it will be quite safe with you."

"Oh, perfectly safe, safe as in the Bank of England. I'm one of your sound men. Sound, and straight, and square, all round—everything you can desire, you know. Everyone trusts me. A man of substance, a man of means—and with a head for business."

"I will ask father when I see him."

"That is right. It will be a little relief. You are a good girl, I always said you were, and had your heart in the right place. You will write to your father to-morrow."

Pasco Pepperill was comparatively genial, even boastful, on the rest of the way. When he arrived at Coombe Cellars, his wife heard the wheels and came to the door. She received Kate without cordiality, and took her husband's little bag of clothes he had taken with him. Kate carried hers in her hand.

"Anything in the cart? Shall I open?" asked Zerah.

"Nothing—absolutely nothing. Leave the cart alone," answered Pasco hastily. "Nothing at all."

Pepperill drew his horse away, unharnessed it, and ran the dog-cart into the coach-house. Then he stood for a moment musing, and looking at it. Presently he turned his back, locked the door, and left his conveyance undischarged of its load of shavings.

"I may chuck 'em away, any time," said he, "or give 'em to Zerah to kindle her kitchen fire with, or"— He did not finish the sentence, even in thought.

CHAPTER XXV
BORROWING AGAIN

When Pepperill, tired with his long day's journey, and harassed in mind, went to his bedroom, Zerah at once fell upon him.

"How have you fared, I'd like to know? But lawk! what's the good of my axing, when I'm pretty confident your journey has been all down hill, with an upset of the cart presently."

"And if it be so, who is to blame but your brother?" retorted Pepperill angrily.

"My brother may have made his mistakes sometimes, but not always—you never by any chance fail to do the wrong thing."

"He has dragged me into this confounded affair of the Brimpts timber; and now—I cannot sell the bark or the oaks."

"He had nothing to say to the wool. What made you buy at a wrong price?"

"The market is always changing."

"Yes—against your interests. We shall end in the workhouse."

"Things will come right."

"They cannot. Look here! Here is a lawyer's letter about the coals. You must pay by the first of the next month, or they will put in the bailiffs."

"It will come right. I have had an offer."

"For the oak?"

"No, of a loan. Kate, like a good and reasonable and affectionate girl, is going to get Jason to withdraw her money and lend it to me."

Zerah flushed crimson. "So!" she exclaimed, planting herself in front of her husband, and lodging her hands on her hips; "you want to swindle the orphan out of her little fortune. You know as well as I do, if that money gets into your hands, it will run between your fingers as has all other money that ever got there. Folks say that there is a stone as turns all base metal to gold. I say that your palm has the faculty of converting gold into quicksilver, that escapes and cannot be recovered."

"This is only a temporary embarrassment."

"It shall not be done," said Zerah. "I don't myself believe Jason will hear of it, and if he does, and prepares to carry it out, I'll knock his head off—that's my last word. The parson said I didn't love Kate, that I was starving her; but I'll stand up for her against you—and her own father if need be."

"The coal merchant must wait," said Pasco, shrugging his shoulders.

"He will not wait. You have passed over unnoticed his former demands, and now, unless in a fortnight the money is paid, he will make the house too hot to hold us."

"We can sell something."

"What? You have parted with your farm, the orchard, the meadow—with everything but the house, to follow your foolish passion to be a merchant."

"He must wait. I have to wait till folk pay me my little bills. Money doesn't come in rushes, but in leaks."

"He will not wait. Where is the ready money to come from?"

Pasco scratched his head.

"If everything else fails," said she further, "then I propose you go to old Farmer Pooke and get a loan of him."

"Pooke? he won't lend money."

"I am not so sure of that. Jan has called several times since Kitty has been away, and yesterday he told me, in his shy, awkward fashion, that he had spoken with his father about her. The old man made some to-do—he had fancied Rose Ash as a match for his son, as she is likely to have a good round sum of money; but when Jan insisted, he gave way. You see everyone in the place knows that Kate has something left by her mother, but they don't know how much, and, instead of three hundred pounds or so, they have got the notion into their heads that it is a thousand pounds. Now, as the father is ready to let his son marry Kate, I think it like enough he would help you, so as to prevent the scandal of bailiffs in Coombe Cellars."

"He may make that the excuse for breaking off the match."

"Jan is obstinate. When that lad sets his head on a thing, there is no turning him, and that his father knows well. He'd ha' turned his son away from Kitty and on to Rose if he could, but he can't do it; and what he is aware of is, that the least show of opposition will make Jan ten times more set on it than before."

"Then you go to Farmer Pooke and borrow."

"I! I made to go round as a beggar-woman! You have brought trouble on the house. You must ask for the loan."

Next day, Pasco Pepperill started for Pooke's house. The lion is said to lash itself with its tail till it lashes itself into fury. Pasco blustered and bragged with everyone he encountered, till he had worked himself up into self-confidence and assurance enough for his purpose, and then, with bold face and swaggering gait, entered the farm-house.

Pooke senior was a stout man, as became a yeoman of substance; he had a red, puffed face, with stony dark eyes; his hands were enormous, and their backs were covered with hair.

Pooke and Pepperill had not been on the best of terms. Pooke for some time had been churchwarden, but in a fit of pique had thrown up the office, when Pepperill had been elected in his room. But Pooke had not intended his resignation to be accepted seriously. He had withdrawn to let the parish feel that it had absolutely no one else fit to take his place, and he had anticipated that he would have been entreated to reconsider his resignation. When, however, Pepperill stepped into his vacant office, and everything went on as usual, Pooke was very irate, and spoke of the supplanter with bitterness and contempt.

"How do y' do?" said Pooke, and extended his hand with gracious condescension, such as he only used to the rector and to those whom he considered sufficiently well-off to deserve his salutation. "What have you come here about?—that matter of Jan?"

"Well, now," answered Pepperill, with a side look at a servant, "between ourselves, you know, we are men who conduct business in a different way from the general run."

"Get along with you, Anne," said Pooke to the maid. "Now we are by ourselves, what is it? That boy Jan is headstrong. It runs in the blood. I married, clean contrary to my father's wishes, just because I knew he didn't like the girl. I don't think that it was anything else made me do it. But your niece, Kitty, has money."

"Money? oh, of course! We are a moneyed family."

"That is well. Mine is a moneyed family. One cannot be comfortable oneself without money, nor have anything to do comfortably with other people unless they're moneyed. I have often thought there is a great gulf fixed between the comfortably off and those who are in poor circumstances, and those who are in comfort can't pass to the other side—not right they should; let them make their associates among the comfortably off. That's my doctrine."

"And mine also," said Pasco. "I like to hear you talk like this—it's wholesome."

"Well, and what do you want with me?"

Pepperill crossed his legs, uncrossed them, and crossed them again.

"I've been doing a lot o' business lately," said he.

"So I hear. But do you want to do business with me? I bought your orchard and meadow. There I think you did wrong. Hold on to land; never let that go—that's my doctrine. You got rid of it, and where are you now? In Coombe Cellars, without as much as five acres around it of your own."

"I never was calculated to be a farmer," said Pasco. "My head was always set on a commercial life, and I can't say I regret it. A lot of money has passed through my hands."

"I don't care so much for the passing as the sticking of money," retorted Pooke.

"Well, in my line, money comes in with a tide and goes out with a tide. When it is out, it is very much out indeed; but I have only to wait awhile, and, sure as anything in nature, in comes the tide once more."

Pooke's stony eye was fixed on Pepperill.

"Which is it now—high tide or low water?"

"There it is—low."

"Oh!"

Pooke thrust his chair back, and looked at the space between him and Pepperill, as though it were the great gulf fixed, across which no communication was possible.

"Merely temporary," said Pasco, with affected indifference. "Nevertheless, unpleasant rather; not that I am inconvenienced and straitened myself, but that I am unable to extend my money ventures. You see, I have been buying a great oak wood on Dartmoor—splendid oak, hard as iron; will make men-of-war, with which we shall bamboozle the French and Spaniards. Then I've bought in a quantity of wool."

"What, now? It is worth nothing."

"Exactly—because there is a panic. In my business this is a time for buying. There will be a rebound, and I shall sell. It is the same with coals. I lay in now when cheap, and sell when dear—in winter."

"What do you want with me?" asked Pooke suspiciously.

"The thing is this. I find I have to pay for the timber before I can sell a stick to Government, and I haven't the cash at this instant. I've had to pay for the wool,—I bought in two years' fleeces,—and for the coals, and if I could lay my hand on four hundred pounds"—

"Four hundred pound ain't things easy laid hands on."

"I want the money for three months at the outside. I'll give you my note of hand, and what interest you demand."

"Likely to make a good thing out of Government? I've always heard as dealing with Government is like dealing with fools—all gain your side, all loss theirs."

"Well! 'Tis something like that," said Pepperill, with a knowing wink. "But don't trouble yourself; if you can't conveniently raise four or five hundred, I can easily go elsewhere. I came to you, because my wife said there was likely to be a marriage between the families, and so I thought you might help me to make this hit."

"Now, look here," said Pooke. "I've often had a notion I should like to deal with Government. I've a lot of hay and straw."

"I'm your man. Trust me. If I get to deal with Government about the timber, they'll have confidence in me, for the oak is about first-rate, and no mistake. They'll become confiding, and I'll speak a word for you. But if you haven't any loose cash, such as four or five hundred pounds"—Pepperill stood up, and took his hat.

"Don't go in a hurry," said Pooke. "That's been my ambition, to deal with Government. Then if one has mouldy hay, one can get rid of it at a good figure, and Government is so innocent, it will buy barley straw for wheaten."

"If you are so hard up that you have no money"—

"I—I hard up? Sit down again, Pasco."

Pooke considered for a moment, and then said, "Now, I know well enough that in business matters sometimes one wants a loan. It is always so. If you'll just give me a leg up with Government, I don't mind accommodating you. But—I must have security."

"On my stores?"

"No; they might sell out. On your house."

"Won't my note of hand do?"

"No, it won't," answered Pooke. "See here: my Jan has gone down your way to make it up with Kitty. When they have settled, you get me your deeds, and then I don't mind advancing the sum you want on that security—that is, if Kitty accepts Jan."

"She will do so, of course," said Pepperill.

"Well, of course," said Pooke.

CHAPTER XXVI

SILVER PENINKS

As soon in the morning as Kate could disengage herself from the tasks which her aunt at once imposed on her, she ran to the cottage occupied by the wife and children of Roger Redmore. It was of cob, or clay and straw beaten and trampled together, then shaved down, and the whole thatched.

Such cottages last for centuries, and are warm and dry. So long as the thatch is preserved over the walls, there is simply no saying how long they may endure, but if the rain be suffered to fall on the top of the walls, the clay crumbles rapidly away. The cob is usually whitewashed, and the white faces of these dwellings of the poor under the brown velvet-pile thatched roofs, with the blinking windows beneath the straw thatching just raised, like the brow of a sleepy eye, have an infinitely more pleasing, cosy appearance than the modern cottages of brick or stone, roofed with cold blue slate.

The cottage of the Redmores was built against a red hedge, rank with hawthorn and primroses. But in verity it was no longer the cottage of the Redmores, for the family had been given notice to quit, and although after Lady-Day Farmer Pooke had suffered the woman to inhabit it for a few weeks, yet now the term of his concession was exceeded. He had a new workman coming in, and the unhappy woman was forced to leave.

When Kate arrived at the dwelling, she found that some sympathetic neighbours were there, who were assisting Jane Redmore to remove her sticks of furniture from the interior. The labourer who was incomer was kindly, and also lent a hand. Her goods had been brought out into the lane, and were piled up together against the bank, and on them she sat crying, with her children frightened and sobbing around her. Neighbours had been good to her, and now endeavoured to appease the tears and distress of the children with offers of bread and treacle, and bits of saffron cake, and endearments. The woman herself was helpless; she did not know whither she should betake herself for the night, where she should bestow her goods.

The incomer urged Mrs. Redmore to tell him what were her intentions. He must bring in his own family that afternoon, and would help her, as much as he was able, to settle herself somewhere. It was not possible for her to remain in the road. The parish officers would interfere, and carry her off to the poorhouse; but it was uncertain whether she could be accommodated there, interposed a neighbour, as the house was full of real widows.

Mrs. Redmore was a feeble, incapable creature, delicate, without the mental or moral power of rising to an emergency and forming a resolution. She sat weeping and crying out that she was without Roger, and he always managed for her.

"But you see, Jane," argued a neighbour, "as how Roger can't be here for very good reasons, which us needn't mention, and so someone must do something, and who else is there but you?"

"I wish I was dead," wailed the poor creature.

"Well, now, Jane," said the neighbour, "don't ye be so silly. If you was dead, what 'd become o' the childer?"

At this juncture Kate arrived, breathless with running.

"It is well." She stood panting, with her eyes bright with pleasure at the consciousness that she brought relief. "I asked my father, and he says Mrs. Redmore and the little ones may go into his cottage at Roundle Post, and stay there till something is settled."

"That's brave!" exclaimed the women who were standing round. "Now, let me take the little ones, Jane, and you lead the way, and Matthew Woodman, he'll help to carry some of your things."

"I have the key," said Kate; "and the distance is nothing."

"Lawk a mussy!" exclaimed one of the women; "what would us ever a' done wi'out you, Kitty. The poor creetur is that flummaged and mazed, her don't seem right in her head, and us couldn't do nothing with she."

Mrs. Redmore caught Kate's hand, and kissed it.

"We'd all a' died here, but for you," she said.

"Indeed," answered Kate, hastily snatching her hand away, "it is my father who has come to your assistance not I. He lends you the house."

"But you axed him for it. Oh, if Roger could do anything for you!"

"I assure you my father is the one to be thanked, if anyone is."

"Well, if Roger could do aught for he, it would be the same as to you."

"Come, let us be on the move."

A little procession formed—women carrying the children, or crocks, a couple of men with wheelbarrows, removing some of the heavier goods. Then up came Jan Pooke, and at once offered his assistance, and worked as hard as any.

As soon as the poor woman was settled into her new quarters, Jan sidled up to Kate, and, seizing her hand and breathing heavily, said, "Kitty, I want to say something to you."

The girl looked at him inquiringly, waiting for what he had to say.

"I mean, Kitty, alone."

"I am Kitty Alone," observed she, with a smile.

"I don't mean that. I have something I want to say to you."

"What is it?" said she. "You look very odd."

"It's—it's—the silver peninks."

"What of them?"

It must be premised that the "silver peninks" are the *narcissus poeticus.*

"They are in an orchard."

"I know it," said Kate. "Lovely they are—and yet, somehow, I like the daffodils as well."

"Now, it's a curious thing," said Jan, "that the same roots bring up first daffies, and then silver peninks."

"That is not possible," objected Kate.

"But it is so. Come into the orchard, Kitty, and see for yourself."

"I know, without seeing, that it cannot be."

"If you will come and look, Kitty, you will see that just where the daffies were, there the peninks are now. When the daffies die down, the peninks bloom."

"Exactly, Jan, because their time for blooming is a month later than the daffodils."

"But they come out of the same roots."

"That cannot be, by any means."

Pooke rubbed his head, and said humbly, "I know, Kitty, I'm a duffer, and that you're clever, but I've seen 'em with my own eyes."

"Have you ever dug up the bulbs?"

"No, I can't say I have done that."

"Till you have, you cannot say that the golden flower and the silver flower spring from one root."

"It isn't only the peninks, Kitty—can't you understand?"

"I do not. You are very wonderful to-day."

"I want to talk to you in the orchard."

"You can say what it is, here."

"No, I cannot. I want to show you the silver peninks, and I want to say"—he let go her hand, with which he had been sawing.

Kate looked round. It would be considerate to leave the poor woman alone with her children to get settled into her new quarters, and she desired to escape another outburst of gratitude.

"Well, Jan, I will go and look at the flowers, and I hope to show you your mistake—the withered heads of daffodil apart from the bursting bud of the penink."

The two young people walked together down the lane to the gate into the orchard. Jan threw this open, and Kate, without hesitation, stepped in.

"Now," said Jan, "I said it was not the peninks."

"What is not the peninks—the daffodils? I thought you said that the one plant was the same which throws up yellow flowers and white ones."

"You try not to understand me, Kitty."

"I am trying hard to understand you, Jan."

"Look here," he exclaimed, letting go the gate. Kate did as desired; she looked him full in the face. His mouth was twitching. "Tell me, Kate"—

She waited for him to conclude the sentence, and as he did not, she asked him gently what it was that he desired her to tell him.

"You know already what I mean," he exclaimed, breathing short and quick.

Kate shook her head.

"Look here, Kitty. My father has given his consent at last, and I am going to be married."

"I am so glad to hear it, Jan."

"Kate, you tease me. You—you"—

"Indeed, I wish you all happiness."

"That I can only have with you."

"With me?" Kate was frightened, drew back, and fixed her great, dark blue, tranquil eyes on him. The sweat rolled off his brow.

"Oh, Jan! What do you mean?"

"You know what I mean. You shall be my missus."

"Jan—that cannot be."

"Why not? Give me your hand—no, give me both."

"I cannot do that."

A pause ensued.

"Kitty, you don't care for me?"

"I do care for you, Jan."

"Then love me—take me. Sister Sue will be so pleased."

"I cannot do it, Jan, even for sister Sue."

"You cannot love me?" he gasped, and his face lost its colour. "Oh, Kitty, since we were in the boat together I have thought only of you."

"And before that, of Rose. Was it not so?"

"No, Kitty. Rose rather teased me."

"Jan, you are a dear, good old fellow, and I like you better than any—I mean, almost better than anyone else in the world."

"Whom do you like better?" he inquired in a tone between sulk and anger.

"My dear father, of course."

"Oh, your father!—anyone else?"

"I love the dear old parson."

"The parson? why so?"

"Because one can learn so much from him."

"Oh, learn, learn!" exclaimed Pooke impatiently. "At that rate you will love the schoolmaster, for he can teach you all sorts of things—why some stars twinkle and others do not; and why the tides do not come regular by half an hour. If that sort of foolery suits you, he'll do."

"It is no foolery, dear friend Jan. I have said that I did regard and like you." Her face had become crimson.

"But you will not love me."

"Jan, I shall always think of you as a brother or a cousin. You are so good, so true, so kind. You deserve the best girl in Coombe, and I am not that."

He wanted to interrupt her, but she proceeded, laying her finger-tips on his breast.

"No, Jan, I am not that—I know it well; and I know that your father, not even sister Sue, would have you marry me. I cannot love you, and you would be unhappy with me."

"Why that?"

"Because I would be for ever asking you questions which you could not answer. And I, with you, would not be happy, because I could get no answers out of you. You would be telling me such things as that silver peninks sprang out of daffodil roots, and that—I could not believe."

"So you refuse me?"

"Jan, you must get a good dear wife, who will believe that silver peninks grow out of daffodil bulbs—will not bother whether they do or not—one who loves you with her whole heart. I know one who does that—no—listen to me!" as he made a gesture of impatience, as if he would turn away. "Let me speak plainly, Jan. Rose is a merry, good-hearted girl; and if she has done an unkind thing to me, it has not been out of malice, but because it made her mad to think that you did not love her, and cared a little for me. No one in Coombe can say a bad word against her. She is the prettiest girl in all the country round. She is always neat and fitty (dapper). If you know at all what love is, Jan, you must judge how miserable Rose is, when, loving you with all her heart, she finds you indifferent, and even rough towards her; she hates me, only because you prefer me to her. Your father, I am quite sure, has no wish to see you marry anyone but Rose. Sister Sue is her friend, and Sue knows and cares nothing about me. Let us always remain friends. I shall ever value you for your goodness of heart, dear Jan. I wish I could love you enough to accept you, but I cannot—I cannot, Jan—and after saying that silver peninks"—

"Oh, confound the peninks!" he used a worse word than "confound."

"Jan! Do not say that. It is a necessity of my heart to learn. I must ask questions, and I never can love a man who cannot give me something to satisfy my mind. Dear Jan, if we were married, and you said that silver"—

He stamped his feet.

"Well, never mind the peninks. It cannot be, Jan. It cannot be. We were never created for each other. Woman is made out of a rib of the man to whom she must belong. If I am so eager to ask questions, and get to know things, that shows, Jan, I was never made out of your rib, never taken from your side, and so never can go there."

CHAPTER XXVII

TROUBLE

When Kate returned to Coombe Cellars, she saw that some trouble had occurred. Her aunt was sitting at the table in tears, Pasco had planted himself on the settle, with his legs stretched before him, wide apart, the soles turned up and his hands in his pockets. His hat was on and he was whistling a tune—a strain out of Jackson's "Tee-dum"—in unconcern.

Kate had heard enough of the altercations between her aunt and uncle to be aware that their circumstances were strained, and that Zerah disbelieved in her husband's business capacities. Pasco had himself admitted to her, on the drive from Brimpts, that he was in difficulties.

Zerah, so far from refraining from her comments before Kate, hailed her entrance as an opportunity for renewing her animadversions on Pasco.

"Look here, Kitty! Here is what we have come to—read that! Your uncle, like a reckless fool, has gone and bought wool when there is no sale for it, and has given a bill for it which has expired. The bank has returned it to Coaker, dishonoured,—dishonoured, do you hear that, Pasco?—and here is Coaker, furious, and demanding immediate payment. On the other side, there is the Teignmouth coal merchant threatening proceedings. What is to be done?"

Kate looked at her uncle.

"Don't be excited and angry, Zerah," said he, with the utmost composure. "After rain comes sunshine. It is darkest before dawn. When the tide is at lowest ebb, it is on the turn to the flow."

"But what is to be done? Dishonoured!" exclaimed Zerah.

"Dishonoured?—fiddlesticks! The bill is returned, that is all. The money will come."

"Whence. Can you stamp on the ground and make the coin leap up? Can you throw your net into the Teign and gather guineas as you can shrimps?"

"It will come right," said Pasco. "There is no need for this heat, I tell you. I have seen Farmer Pooke, and he will advance me five hundred pounds."

"Yes—on the security of this house."

"Well, what of that?"

"And five hundred pounds will not suffice to meet all the claims."

"Well, there are Kitty's hundreds."

"They shall not be touched."

"You promised me the loan of them, did you not, Kitty?" asked her uncle, scarcely raising his head to look at her.

"Yes, you are heartily welcome to them," said the girl.

"They shall not be touched!" exclaimed Zerah, leaning her fists on the table.

"That is as Jason thinks and chooses," answered Pasco. "He is trustee for Kitty, not you. He got me into the hobble, and must get me out."

"What!—did he get you into this about the wool?"

"I should have managed about the wool, were it not for the Brimpts business."

"And the coals?" asked Zerah ironically.

"I can manage well enough when not drawn away into foreign speculations. Jason persuaded me against my will to embark in this timber business, and that is it which is creating this obstruction. He got me in—he must get me out. Kate's a good girl,—she helps, and don't rate and rant as you do, Zerah."

"I don't say she is not a good girl," retorted Zerah. "What I say is, you are a bad uncle to desire to rob her"—

"Rob her? I ask only a loan for a few weeks. Her money and that from Pooke will set us on our feet again."

At that moment, the man just alluded to came in with much noise. His face was red, his expression one of great anger, and without a greeting, he roared forth—

"It is an insult. The girl is an idiot. She has refused him—him—a Pooke!"

"Who? What?" asked Zerah, letting go the table and staggering back, overcome by a dreadful anticipation of evil.

"Who? What?" retorted Pooke, shaking his red face and then his great flabby hand at Kate. "She—Kitty Alone—has said No to my John!"

Zerah uttered an exclamation of dismay. Pasco's jaw fell, and, drawing in his feet, he pulled his hands from his pockets and leaned them on the arms of the settle, to be ready to lift himself.

"She—that chit—has dared to refuse him!" roared Pooke. "Not that I wanted her as my daughter. Heaven defend! I think my John is worth better girls than she. But that she should have refused him—my John—she who ought to have gone down on her knees and thanked him if he gave her a look—that she should have the impudence—the—the"—he choked with rage. "Now, not one penny of mine shall you have, not on note of hand, on no security of your beggarly house—a cockle and winkle eating tea-house—bah!—not a penny!"

Then he turned, snapped his fingers at Zerah and Pasco, and went out.

There ensued a dead hush for some moments. Kate had turned very white, and looked with large frightened eyes at her uncle, then at her aunt. She felt that this was but the first puff of a storm which would break in full force on her head.

Pasco stumbled to his feet, planted his right fist in the hollow of his left palm, and, coming up close to Kate, said hoarsely, "You won't have him? You, you frog in a well! You won't have him, the richest young chap in Coombe! I say you shall have him. You shall run after Mr. Pooke, and say it is all a mistake—you take Jan thankfully—you only said No just out of bashfulness, you did not think yourself worthy. Tell him you said No because you thought Jan was asking you against his father's wishes. Say that now you know how the old man feels, you gratefully accept. Do you hear? Run."

Kate did not move. Her head had fallen on her bosom when he began, now she raised it, and, looking her uncle steadily in the face, she said, "I cannot. I have told Jan my reasons."

"Reasons, indeed! precious reasons. What are they?"

Kate did not answer. Her reasons were such as Pasco could not understand.

"Kate," interposed Zerah in an agitated voice, "what is the meaning of this?"

"Oh, dear aunt, it is true, I cannot take Jan. I have refused him, and I cannot, will not withdraw the No. In this matter I alone am answerable, and answerable to God."

"I insist," stormed Pasco.

"I cannot obey," answered Kate.

"Cannot—will not obey us who have brought you up. I suppose next you will refuse to obey your father?"

"In this matter, yes, if he were to order me to take Jan Pooke."

"I'll force you to take him."

"You cannot do that, uncle." She spoke with composure, whereas he was in a towering passion.

"Look at this," said he, snatching up the letter from the table. "I'm dishonoured now, indeed, as Zerah says. If you take Jan, all is well. The old father will find me money, and all runs on wheels. You put in your spoke, and everything is upset. Dishonoured, ruined, beggared—and all through you."

He beat down his hat over his brows, laughed wildly, and shook his fist at Kate. "I was chucked out of the trap t'other day. I wish I had broken my neck sooner than come to this. I've nourished a viper in my bosom, and now it turns and stings me."

"Leave her to me," said Zerah. "You make matters worse by your violence. That is the way with you men. Leave her to me."

Pasco flung himself back in the settle, and thrust out his legs as before, and rammed his fists into his pockets. Before he had held his chin up, now it was buried in his shirt front.

Then Zerah pulled her niece into the window. Kate drew a long breath. She knew that now came the worst trial of all.

"Kitty," said the aunt, holding both the girl's arms, and looking into her face. "Are you utterly heartless? Is it a matter of no concern to you that we should be ruined? You have but to run after Mr. Pooke, and all will be well. Why should you not give way to my wishes and those of your uncle? What have you against the lad? He is good, and he is rich."

"I do not love him," answered Kate confusedly.

"But he is so well off. There is no one with half his prospects in the place. I can't understand. He likes you. He is desperately fond of you."

"I will never take one I do not love," said Kate, shaking her head.

"And you have heard the condition we are in? Your uncle owes money on all sides. If money is due to him, he cannot recover it. He has sold the farm, there remains only this house. If he sells that, we are without a home. Then where will you be? Come—yield to our wishes, child."

"I cannot, indeed I cannot," answered Kate, trembling in all her limbs. "I would have taken Jan if I could."

"What is to prevent you?"

Kate was silent.

"There is—there can be no one else in the way?" pursued Zerah.

Again no answer.

"Stubborn and hardhearted, that is what you are," said Zerah bitterly. "It is all the same to you what becomes of us. We reared you. We have loved you. I have been to you as a mother. You have never shown either your uncle or me that you were grateful for what we have done for you. Your own father you treat as though he were a dog—take no notice of him. I have heard of hearts of stone, I never believed in them before. I do now. No; there is—there can be no one else so insensible. You have not got it in you to love anyone."

Kate sighed. The tears ran down her cheeks.

"Dear aunt, I have always loved you, and I love you now, and ever will."

"Then show me that you have a heart," said Zerah. "Words without deeds are wind. If my own dear child Wilmot had been alive, this would not have happened. Jan would have loved her, not you; and even if she had not cared for him, yet, when she knew my wishes, she would have yielded. She would have given her heart's blood for me."

Kate pressed her folded hands to her bosom; her heart was bursting with pain.

"What is it that I ask of you?" pursued Zerah, and brushed the tears from her own eyes. "Nothing but what is for your own advantage, your own happiness. How will you like starvation—rags, no roof over your head? If you take Jan Pooke, you become the first woman in the place. You will have money to do with just as you likes. Jan is a good-hearted fellow. Never have you heard of his having wronged man, woman, or child. He is amiable; you can turn him round your little finger. What more can a woman wish for?"

Kate's mind was tossed with trouble. She had so often longed that the opportunity might arise for her to prove to her aunt that she loved her. Now the occasion had come. The future was full of threat and disaster, and one word from her might avert this and restore serenity; and not only would that one word relieve her uncle and aunt in their present distress, but it would also suffice to make poor, worthy Jan a happy man. But that word she could not speak, she could not prevail with herself to speak it. She liked John Pooke, and but for one thing she perhaps might have yielded—that one thing was that she had met with a man very different from the young yeoman, one who could answer questions and satisfy her hungry mind.

"I cannot, dear auntie."

"Cannot? What stands in the way? *Who* stands in the way?"

"I cannot, auntie."

"Perverse, headstrong, heartless child! When luck comes to you, you throw it away, and cast your own self, and all belonging to you, into misery. I wish you had never come here; I wish I had never nursed you in my arms, never cared for you as a child, never watched over you as a grown girl."

"Auntie!"

"Away—I will not speak to you again."

CHAPTER XXVIII

ALTERNATIVES

Pasco had left the room and the house. His anger with Kate was obscured by his unrest as to his own condition. What could he do?

He must meet the bill for the wool, he must pay for the Brimpts timber before he removed any of it, or forfeit what had already been spent over felling the trees. He must pay the coal merchant's account, or bailiffs would be put into the house.

He went into his stores and observed the contents of his warehouse. There was wool on the upper storey, coal was lodged below. Above stairs all the space was pretty well filled with fleeces.

Then he went to his stable, and looked at his cob, then into the covered shed that served as coach-house. He put his hand in his pocket, pulled out the key, and opened the back of the cart. The shavings he had put in were there still. He could not carry them into the house now, whilst Zerah was engaged with Kate. Besides, he would not require so much kindling matter within doors. Where should he bestow it?

Suspecting that he heard a step approach, Pasco hastily closed the flap of the cart, and went to the front of the shed. No one was there. He returned to the shed and reopened the box of the cart, and filled his arms with shavings, came out and hastily ran across with them to his warehouse.

Then he came back on his traces, carefully picking up the particles that had escaped him. There remained more in his dog-cart. Would it do for him to run to and fro, conveying the light shavings from shed to warehouse? Might it not attract attention? What would a customer think were he to come for coals, and find a bundle of kindling wood among them? What would neighbours think at the light curls caught by the wind and carried away over the fields?

He went hastily back to the warehouse and collected the bundle he had just taken there, and brought it all back in a sack, and rammed this sack into the box of his cart; and then went again to the stores, and raked the coals over the particles of shavings that remained.

Then Pasco harnessed his cob, and drove away to the little town of Newton. A craving desire had come over him to see again the new public-house erected in the place of that which had been burnt. He had no clear notion why he desired to see it.

As he drove along, he passed the mill, and Ash, the miller, who was standing outside his house, hailed him.

"By the way, Pepperill—sorry to detain you; there is a little account of mine I fancy has been overlooked. Will you wait?—I will run in and fetch it; my Rose—she does all the writing for me, I'm a poor scholard—she has just made it out again. It was sent in Christmas, and forgot, I s'pose, then again Lady-Day, and I reckon again overlooked. You won't mind my telling of it, and if you could make it convenient to pay"—

"Certainly, at once," answered Pasco, and thrust his hand into his pocket and drew it forth empty. "No hurry for a day or two, I reckon? I find I have come away without my purse."

"Oh no, not for a day or two; but when it suits you, I shall be obliged."

"Will to-morrow do?"

"Of course. I say, Pepperill, your brother-in-law is a right sort of a man."

"Why do you say that?"

"Giving up his cottage to that poor creetur, Jane Redmore."

"I do not understand you."

"What—have you not heard? There was like to be a proper mess. Farmer Pooke wanted Roger's cottage for his new man, and so she, poor soul, had to turn out. There was no help for it. She had no notion where to go, and what to do. A lost sort of creetur I always thought, and now that Roger is away and not to be found, and what wi' the death of her little maid, gone almost tottle (silly). Her had to clear out, and folks was nigh mazed to know what to do wi' her, when your niece, Kitty Alone, came and said as how her father Jason gave his cottage till Jane Redmore could settle something."

"I never heard a word of this till this moment," said Pasco. "When did it happen?"

"To-day—not long ago. Jane Redmore is in Jason Quarm's house now. Kate gave her the key."

Pepperill grew red, and said, not looking Ash in the face, but away at the ears of his horse, "I don't like this—not at all. We ought to get rid of Redmore and all his belongings. You are not safe in your house, your mill is not safe, I am not safe, with that firebrand coming and going amongst us—and come and go he will so long as his wife and children be here. He were mighty fond of they."

"Roger will do you no harm. Your people have been good to him."

"What! do you call Jason 'my people'?"

"Jason and Kitty have housed his wife."

"It don't follow that he loves me. I set the men in pursuit of him at Dart-meet, and he knows it, and hates me. I live in fear of him as long as he is uncaught."

The miller shrugged his shoulders. "Roger is not so bad, but Farmer Pooke did try him terrible. I won't detain you. You'll mind and pay that little account, will you not—to-morrow?"

"Yes—certain."

Then Pepperill drove on. He passed a man in a cart, and the man did not salute him. In fact, the way was narrow, and the fellow was careful that the wheels should clear, and had not leisure to look at and touch his hat to Pasco. But Pepperill regarded the omission as an intentional slight. He was in an irritable condition, and when shortly after he drove before a cottage, and the woman in the doorway, hushing her child, did not address him, or answer his address, his brows knitted and he swore that everyone was against him. His disturbed and anxious mind longed for recognition, flattery, to give it ease, and unless he received this from everyone, he suspected that there was a combination against him, that a wind of his difficulties had got abroad, and that folk considered he was no longer worth paying attention to.

There were not many on the road, and he acted capriciously towards those few. Some he greeted, others he passed without notice. He fancied he detected a sneer in the faces of such as returned his salutation or a purposeful lessening of cordiality. On reaching the new inn at Newton, his heart was full of anger against all mankind.

The host did not receive him with cordiality, as he expected; he looked out at the door and went in again with a hasty nod.

In the yard Pasco cautiously opened his gig-box when the ostler was not looking and drew out a halter, then, hastily closed the flaps, and, extending the cord, said, "I'm not going to stay many minutes; don't take the cob out of harness. Let him stand and eat a bite, that is all."

Then Pepperill went into the inn and called for a glass of ale.

"Halloa, Pepperill!" said a cheery voice, and Coaker moved up to him at the table. "How are you? Sold the wool yet? I hear there is a rise."

Pepperill drew back and turned blood-red; this was the man to whom he owed so much money—the man to whom he had given the bill that was dishonoured.

"No, I haven't sold," answered Pasco surlily.

"I advise you not to. You'll make something yet. That Australian wool won't go down with our weavers. It's not our quality, too fine, not tough enough. Hold back, and you will make your price."

"That is all very well for you to say, but"— Pasco checked himself. What was on his lips was—"It is ready-money I need, not a profit a few months hence."

"There's good things coming to you yet," continued Coaker. "I heard on the moor that your brother-in-law has near on made a sale of the Brimpts oaks."

"He has?"

"Yes; there has been a timber merchant from Portsmouth come there. He wanted the Okehampton oaks, but was too late, they had been picked up, so he came on to Dart-meet, and I reckon now it is only about price they are haggling, that is all." Coaker dropped his voice and said, "There's an awkwardness about that bill of yours. Nay, don't kick out; I won't be so terrible down on you just for a fortnight or three weeks. I'll let you turn that timber over first if you will be sharp about it. There, don't say I'm down on you. A fortnight or three weeks I give you."

Pasco held up his head, but the sudden elation was damped by the thought that he could not remove any of the timber till the covenanted price had been paid for it, and whence was this money to come? Money he must have to enable him to hold on with the wool till it fetched a better price, and to dispose of the oaks he had felled on the moor, to enable him to escape the scandal and humiliation of having the bailiffs put in his house by the coal merchant.

But then, in the event of a certain contingency which loomed before Pasco's inner eye, there would be no wool to be disposed of, it would have been reduced to—even to himself he would not complete the sentence. Would that matter? The insurance would more than cover the loss, and he would be able to dispose of the oak.

"Will you have a pipe?" asked Coaker, and after having stuffed his tobacco into his bowl, he produced a match-box and struck a light with a lucifer. At the period of this tale lucifer matches were a novelty. The tinder-box was in general use for domestic purposes, and men carried about with them small metal boxes, armed with a steel side, containing amadou and flint, for kindling their pipes and cigars.

"What do you call that?" asked Pepperill, observing the proceedings of the farmer.

"Ah! I reckon this be one of the finest inventions of the times. Have you never seen or read of this yet? It is better than the phosphorus bottle, and than Holmberg's box. Look here. This little stick has got some chemical stuff, sulphur and something else, phosphorus, I believe, at the end; all you have to do is to rub, and the whole bursts into flame."

Pepperill took the box, turned it over, opened it, looked at and smelt the matches.

"Are they terrible expensive?" he asked musingly.

"Oh no. There, as you are curious about it, I'll give you the box, and you can show it to your missus."

Pasco put out his hand to shake that of Coaker. It was cold and trembled.

The devil was playing a game with him. He was offering him a reprieve from his embarrassments, and at the same time thrusting him forward to the accomplishment of the evil deed on which he brooded, and was placing in his hands the means of executing it.

Pasco sank into deep thought, looking at the match-box and playing with it, now opening, then shutting it.

"I'm depriving you of it," he said.

"Not a bit. I have a dozen. They are just brought in from London and are selling off amazin' fast at Ashburton. In a week they'll be all over the country and the tinder boxes chucked away."

"Are they dangerous—I mean to carry about with one?" asked Pasco.

"Not a bit. There is no fire till you strike it out."

Then Pepperill again fell into meditation. He put the box into his pocket, and sat looking before him into space, speechless.

Suddenly a shock went through his frame. He had been touched on the arm by Coaker.

"What is it?" he asked, with quivering lips.

"Look at the landlord," said the farmer in an undertone, with his hand to his mouth. "Do you know what folks say of him?"

Pasco asked with his eyes. He could not frame the words with his lips.

"They do say that he set fire to the old place, so as to get the insurance money for rebuilding in grand style."

"A tramp did it—got into the cellar," said Pasco in a whisper.

"Nobody never saw thickey tramp come, and sure and sartain nobody never saw him go. I don't believe in the tramp. He did it himself."

"You should not speak that unless sure of it," said Pepperill, thrusting back his chair. "You have no evidence."

"Oh, evidence! Folks talk, and form their opinion."

"Talk first and form opinions after on the idle chatter—that's about it."

Pasco stood up. He was alarmed. He was afraid he had not fastened the box of his dog-cart. The flap might have fallen, and then the interior would be exposed to view; and what would the ostler, what would anyone think who happened to come into the stable-yard and saw what constituted the lading of his cart? His hand had shaken as he turned the key, after bringing out the halter; almost certainly in his nervousness he had imperfectly turned it. He could not rest. He went out into the yard and looked at his dog-cart. It was closed. He tried the key. The lock was fast.

"Put the cob in," said he to the ostler, and he returned, much relieved, to the house.

Coaker had departed. Pepperill called for another glass of ale, and found interest in observing the landlord. That man had set fire to his tavern so that he might construct an hotel. He seemed cheery. He was not bowed down with consciousness of guilt. His voice was loud, his spirits buoyant. He looked Pepperill full in the eyes, and it was the eyes of Pepperill that fell, not those of the landlord.

"I wonder," considered Pasco, "whether he did do it, or did not? If he did not, it is just as bad as if he did, for people charge him with it all the same. No one will believe he is innocent. Suppose he did it—and I reckon it is most likely—well, Providence don't seem to ha' turned against him; on the contrary, it is a showering o' prosperity over him. P'r'aps, after all, there ain't no wrong in it. It was his own house he burnt. A man may do what he will with his own." He put resolutely from him the thought of fraud on the insurance company. What was a company? Something impersonal. Then Pepperill rose, paid for his ale, and went forth. As he jumped into the dog-cart, the ostler held up the halter.

"Will you give me the key and I will put it inside?" asked the man.

"No, thank you—hand it to me."

The ostler gave him the halter, and Pepperill fastened it to the splashboard and drove on. He had attached it hastily, carelessly, and before long the rope uncoiled and hung before him. His eyes were drawn to it.

"What would come to me if the bailiffs were put into the house, and Coombe Cellars were sold over my head to pay what I owe?"

Pasco was a man who could live only where he was esteemed, looked up to, and where he could impose on underlings and brag among equals. The idea of being in every man's mouth as "gone scatt"—a ruined man—

was intolerable. "I would die rather than that," he exclaimed aloud, and put his hand to the halter to twist it and knot it again.

It was a sin to commit suicide. His life was his own, but he could not take that. His storehouse with his stores was his own. Would it be wrong for him to destroy that? Better that than his own life. There were but two courses open to him. He must either use the halter for his own neck and swing in the barn, or recover himself out of the insurance money on his stores. He drove on brooding over this question, arguing with his conscience, and presently he held up his head. He saw that his life was too precious to be thrown away. What would Zerah do without him? He must consider his wife, her despair, her tears. He had no right to make her a widow, homeless. Were he to die—that would not relieve the strain. The sale would take place just the same, and Zerah be left destitute. Pepperill held up his head. He felt virtuous, heroic; he had done the right thing for the sake of his dear wife, made his election, and saw a new day dawning—dawning across a lurid glare.

CHAPTER XXIX

A FRIEND GAINED

Kate fled upstairs to her bedroom, where she might be alone and have free scope for tears. She threw herself on her knees by her bed, and putting her hands under the patchwork quilt, drew it over her ears and head, that the sound of her sobs might be muffled, so as not to reach her aunt were she to ascend the staircase. She feared lest there should be a repetition of the scene on the return of her father. Aunt Zerah would wait impatiently for him, and the moment that he arrived, would pour forth her story, not in his ear only, but in Kate's as well, whom she would forcibly retain to hear it and receive the reproaches of her father. That her father would be disappointed that she had put from her the chance of becoming a well-to-do yeoman's wife, she knew for certain. He had never concerned himself very greatly about her, had never endeavoured to sound her mind and put his finger on her heart, and would be quite unable to appreciate the reasons she could give for her conduct; he would look on her refusal of young Pooke as a bit of girlish caprice. She feared that he would view it as a bad speculation, and would hasten off without consulting her, to endeavour to pacify the mortified vanity of the old man, and to assure the young one that she, Kate, had rejected him out of girlish bashfulness, whilst loving him in her heart. There was no bond of sympathy between her father and herself. That which filled his mind had no place in hers; what interested him she shrank from. She had returned from Dartmoor with heart glowing with gratitude to him for having insisted on her having a holiday, to her uncle for having taken her out to Dartmoor, and to her aunt for having spared her. It had been her desire to find occasions to prove to them that she was grateful, and now, her first act on return was to run contrary to their wishes, and anger her uncle and aunt, and lay up matter for reprimand on the arrival of her father.

Her aunt had never comprehended the character of Kate, filled to the full as her heart was with bitterness at the loss of her own daughter. Kate was in all points the reverse of Wilmot, and because so unlike, woke the antipathy of the bereaved mother, as though the silence and reserve of

Kate were assumed out of slight to the memory of the merry, open-hearted girl. She looked on her niece as perverse, as acting in everything out of a spirit of contrariety. How else explain that a young girl with warm blood in her veins should not retain the longings and express the wishes common to other girls of her age? that she had no fancy for dress, made no efforts to coquette with anyone, had no desire for social amusements?

Wilmot had been frolicsome, roguish, winsome—did Kate desire to eschew everything that had made her cousin a sunbeam in the house, and the delight of her mother's heart, out of wilfulness, and determination not to please her aunt, not to make up to her for the loss of her own child?

Not only by her aunt was Kate regarded as heartless and perverse. That was the character she bore in the village, among the girls of her own age, among the elders who adopted the opinions of their daughters. Kate had been brought in contact with the village girls at school, in the choir, and elsewhere, and some had even attempted to make friends with her. But those things which occupied the whole souls of such young creatures—dress, the budding inclination to attract the youths of the place—were distasteful to Kate; there was nothing in common between them and her, and when both became conscious of this, they mutually drew apart, and the girls arrived at the same conclusion as her aunt, that she was a dull, unfeeling child, who was best left alone.

Kate had felt acutely this solitariness in which she lived; her aunt had often thrown it in her teeth that she made no friends. Her father was displeased that he heard no good report of his daughter; her uncle had rudely told her that a girl who made herself so unpopular to her own sex would never attract one of the other. Now the opportunity had come to her to falsify his predictions, to gratify her father, and to make her aunt proud—but she had rejected it, and was more than ever alone. Loneliness was endurable ordinarily. Kitty had her occupations, and, when not occupied, her thoughts, recently her book, to engross her; but now, when her own relatives were against her it was more than she could bear. The pain of desolation became insupportable. There were but two persons she knew with whom she was in touch, two persons only who could feel with and for her, and to one of these she could not fly.

The rector, whom she had loved and respected, was the only friend to whom she could unburden her trouble, and she feared to approach him, because she had just done what he might not like, any more than did her uncle and aunt. He would hear, and that speedily, of her conduct, and

Kate wished greatly to see him, and explain her refusal to him as far as she could, that he might not blame her. But even should her explanation prove unsatisfactory to him, she was not prepared to withdraw her refusal. Kate never wavered. She was one of those direct persons who, when they have taken a course, hold to it persistently.

She rose from her knees, bathed her face, brushed her hair, and descended.

Her aunt was in the kitchen, and averted her face as the girl entered. She did not ask Kate where she was going, nor turn her head to see what she was about.

"I shall be back again in a few minutes, auntie; if you can spare me, I should like to go out."

No answer; and Kate left.

She had not taken many steps from the house, walking with her head down, as the glare of the sun was too strong for her tear-stung eyes, when she was caught, and before she could see in whose arms she was, she was boisterously kissed.

"You are a dear! you are a darling! I shall always love you."

Kitty saw before her Rose Ash, with glowing cheeks and dancing eyes.

"You darling! I never believed it of you, you are so still. I thought you were sly. I am so sorry I misunderstood you; so sorry I did anything or said anything against you. I will never do it again. I will stand your friend; I will fight your battles. And, look here!"

A polished wood workbox was at her feet. She had put it down for the purpose of disengaging her hands to hug Kate.

"Look, Kitty! This is my own workbox. Is it not beautiful? It has a mother-of-pearl escutcheon on it and lock-plate. And it locks—really locks—not make-believe, like some you buy. And, see! pink silk inside. It is for you. I give it to you. It is nearly new. I am not much of a needlewoman, and so have not used it. It is really a hundred times better than that which Noah knocked—I mean, that which the bear danced upon and smashed. And there is a silver thimble in it. I give it you with all my heart—that is to say, with as much heart as I have left to give to anyone."

Kate stepped back in astonishment. What did this mean?

"O Kitty! you really shall no longer be Kitty Alone; it shall be Kitty and Rose. We shall be regular friends. Only think! I was so jealous of you. I thought that Jan Pooke had taken a fancy to you—and I suppose the silly noodle had done so for a bit, but you know he properly belongs to me. We are to make a pair—everyone says so, and his father and sister

Sue wish it; and I'm sure, I'm sure, so do I. But men are cruel giddy, they turn and turn like weathercocks; and just for a while Jan fancied you. But you put him off bravely, you did."

"What have I done to you?" asked Kate.

"My dear, I heard it all. I saw you and Jan going to the orchard, and I was so jealous that I hid myself in the linhay. I got over the hedge and tore my frock in a bramble, but I did not heed it; I slipped in where I could peep and see, and put out my ears and listen. I know everything. I heard how you spoke up for me, and quite right and reasonable too; and how you refused him, and very sensible you was. Just think what a thing it would ha' been, Kitty, if he'd gone right off his head and married you, and then come to his senses and found he had got the wrong one, and it was me all along he should have had. You would never have known happiness after. You never would have enjoyed peace of conscience again. But you were a sensible child, and did what you ought to ha' done, and nobody can't do more than that; nor promise and vow to do more than what is in the catechism. So, now, I'm all for you, and there is my workbox I give you in place of that the bear kicked to pieces. I don't mind telling you now, Kate, that Noah did it. I put him up to it; I told him he was to do it. He didn't like it, but I forced him to it—I mean to knock the workbox from under your arm. He's a good chap is Noah, and now that it is all put right between Jan and me"—

"Is it? Have you spoken with him?"

"Oh no, I can't say that; but you have refused him. It will take him a day or two to steady his head, and then he will come up right again, and we will make it up, and be the better friends in the end. And, what is more, I'll stand friend to you, Kate. I daresay you'd like Noah, and I'll get him to walk you out on Sundays and to sweetheart you."

"I don't want Noah," said Kate, shrinking.

"Oh yes, you do. Every girl must have her young chap. It ain't natural without. I'll speak with him. He's a terrible good chap is Noah; he'll do anything I ask him. I made him knock the workbox under the bear's feet, and if he'd do that much for me, I'm sure you need not be afraid but he'd sweetheart you at my axing. Besides, he'll be tremendous thrown out when he sees me take up with Jan again, and he'll want some one to walk with, and may just as well take you as another."

"No; please, Rose, do not. I had rather be left alone."

"Stuff and fiddlesticks! It is not right that you should be without a sweetheart. You leave all that to me."

"No, dear Rose, no. You be my friend; that suffices."

"It is because I am your friend that I will do a friend's part."

"No, no, Rose."

"Well, you always were queer; I can't understand you. But never mind; we are friends, though you make me a helpless one. What is the good of a friend but to assist a girl to a lover?"

CHAPTER XXX

UNDER THE MULBERRY TREE

Kate disengaged herself from Rose, and hastened to the Rectory. She opened the garden gate. She was a privileged person there, coming when she liked about choir matters, sent messages by her uncle, who was churchwarden, running in when she had a spare hour to look at Mr. Fielding's picture-books, in strawberry time to gather the fruit and eat it, in preserving time to collect his raspberries, currants, plums, for the cook to convert into jams.

She saw the rector sitting under a mulberry tree on his lawn with a book on his lap. He had removed his hat, and the spring air fluttered his silver hair.

He saw Kate at once, and, smiling, beckoned to her to come and sit by him on the bench that half encircled the old tree.

This she would not do, but she stood before him with downcast eyes and folded hands, and said, "Please, sir, I am afraid you will be cross with me."

"I am never that, Kitty."

"No, sir, never." She raised her flashing blue eyes for a moment. "Perhaps you may be vexed with me. I've just gone and done clean contrary to what you said."

"What did I say?"

"You said after my holiday I was to go home, and obey my uncle and aunt in everything."

"I am sure I never said that."

"It was something like it—be obliging and good."

"Well, have you not been obliging and good?"

"No, sir."

"What have you done?"

"I've crossed them, and I fancy father will be cross too."

"What have you done to cross them?"

"Refused Jan Pooke."

The rector drew back against the tree and smiled.

"Refused? I don't quite understand."

"Please, sir, Jan wanted to make me his wife."

"Well?"

"And I said 'No.'"

"You had made up your mind already?"

"I knew I must say 'No.' Do you know, sir, Jan thought that silver peninks came from daffodil roots."

"Oh! and accordingly you could not say 'Yes'?"

"It was silly; was it not?"

"And that was your real, true reason for saying 'No'?"

Kitty looked down.

"You are not angry with me, sir?"

"No. Are your relations so?"

"Yes; uncle and aunt are dreadfully vexed, and that is what has made me cry. I came home wishing to do everything to please them, and the first thing I did was to make them angry and call me a little viper they had brought up in their bosom. You do not think I did wrong? You are not angry also?"

"No; I do not think you could have done otherwise, if you did not care for John Pooke."

"I did, and I do care for John Pooke."

"Then why did you not take him? Only because of the silver peninks?"

"No, sir; not that only. I care for him, but not enough; I like him, but not enough."

"Quite so. You like, but do not love him."

"Yes, that is it." Kate breathed freely. "I did not know how to put it. Do you think I did right?"

The rector paused before he answered. Then he said, signing with his thin hand, "Come here, little Kitty. Sit by me."

He took her hand in his, and, looking before him, said, "It would have been a great thing for this parish had you become John Pooke's wife, the principal woman in the place, to give tone to it, the one to whom all would look up, the strongest influence for good among the girls. I should have had great hopes that all the bread I have strewed upon the waters would not be strewn in vain."

"I thought you wished it," burst forth from the girl, with a sob. "And yet I could not—I could not indeed. Now I have turned everyone against me—everyone but Rose," she added, truthful in everything, exact in all she said.

"No, Kitty, I do not wish it. It is true, indeed, that it would be a rich blessing to such a place as this to have you as the guiding star to all the womanhood in the place, set up on such a candlestick as the Pookes' farm. But I am not so sure that the little light would burn there and not be smothered in grease, or would gutter, and become extinguished in the wind there. The place is good in itself, but not good for you. It might be an advantage to the parish, but fatal to yourself. John Pooke is an honest, worthy fellow, and he has won my respect because he saw your value and has striven to win you. But he is not the man for you. For my little Kitty I hope there will come some one possessed of better treasures than broad acres, fat beeves, and many flocks of sheep; possessed of something better even than amiability of temper."

"What is that, sir?"

"A well-stored intellect—an active mind. Kitty, no one has more regard for young John than myself, but it would have been terrible to you to have been tied to him. 'Thou shalt not plough with an ox and an ass together' was the command of Moses, and we must not unite under one yoke the sluggish mind with that which is full of activity. No, no, Kitty. You acted rightly. The man who will be fitted to be coupled in the same plough with you will be one of another mould. He will be"—

The garden gate opened, and Walter Bramber entered. A twig of laurel caught his sleeve, and he turned to extricate himself, and did not perceive the rector and Kate. A sudden confusion came over the girl, caused—whether by her thoughts, whether by the words of the rector, whether from natural shyness, she could not tell, but she started from the seat and slipped behind the mulberry.

The schoolmaster came up to the rector when called, and found the old man with a smile playing about his lips.

"I have come, sir," said Bramber, "to ask your advice."

"In private?"

"Yes, sir, if you please."

"Then I cannot grant you an audience now. If you will run round the mulberry, you will discover why."

Bramber was puzzled.

"Do what I say. There is someone there, someone who must retire farther than behind a tree if you are to consult me without being overheard."

The schoolmaster stepped aside to go about the mulberry, and saw Kate standing there, leaning against the trunk, holding together her skirts, and looking down.

"Oh!" laughed Walter; "this is the audience! I do not in the least mind a discussion of my concerns before such an one."

"Come out, Kitty! You hear your presence is desired," called Mr. Fielding, and the girl stepped forward. "Take the place where you were before on one side of me, and Mr. Bramber shall sit on the other, and we will enter on the consideration of his affairs. What are they as to complexion, Bramber, sanguine or atrabilious?"

"Not cheerful, I am afraid. I have my troubles and difficulties before my eyes."

"So has Kitty. She comes to me from the same cause." Then he added, "Well, let us hear and consider."

"It concerns Mr. Puddicombe. I do not know what I ought to do, or whether I should do anything. There is an organised opposition to me, and the late schoolmaster is at the bottom of it. I can clearly perceive that not parents only, but children as well, have been worked upon to offer stubborn opposition to all my changes, and to make myself ridiculous. I need not enter into details. There is this feeling of antagonism in the place, and it paralyses me. If the children were left unmanipulated, I could get along and gain their confidence; but at home they hear what their parents say, what is said to their parents, and they come to school with a purpose not to obey me, not to listen to my instructions, and to make my task in every particular irksome and distasteful. I see precisely what Puddicombe is aiming at—to force me to use the cane, not once or twice, but continuously, and to force me to it by making discipline impossible without it. Then he will have a handle against me, and will rouse the parish to hound me out. What am I to do?"

"Have you called on him?"

"No, sir, I have not. I really could not pluck up courage to do so. I hardly know what I could say to him that is pleasant if we did meet."

"You have not yet met him?"

"No. I do not know him by sight."

"He is not a bad fellow; jovial, a sportsman at heart, and his heart was never in the school; it was to be sought in the kennels, in stables, in the ring, anywhere save in class. That was the blemish in the man. His thoroughness was not where it should have been. His centre of gravity was outside the sphere in which it was his duty to turn. But he is not a bad fellow, good-hearted, placable, and only your enemy because his vanity rather than his pocket is touched by his dismissal. I hear he has announced his intention of becoming a Dissenter; but as he hardly ever came to church when he was professedly a Churchman, I do not suppose chapel will see much of him when he professes himself a Nonconformist. It is a great misfortune when a man's interests lie outside his vocation."

"What shall I do, sir?"

"Call on him."

"What shall I say to him?"

"Something that will please him—nothing about the school; nothing about your difficulties."

"I am supremely ignorant of the cockpit and the race-course. It is very hard when two men belonging to different spheres meet; they can neither understand the other."

"My dear young man, that is what I have been experiencing these many years here; we must strive to accommodate ourselves to inferior ways of thinking and speaking, and then, then only, shall we be able to insinuate into the gross and dark minds some spark of the higher life. Kitty, have I your permission to tell Mr. Bramber what it is that you have just communicated to me? It will be public property throughout Coombe in half an hour, if everyone does not know it now, so it will be revealing no secrets."

Kate looked, with a startled expression in her eyes, at the rector. Why should he care to speak of this matter now? Why before Bramber? But she had confidence in him, and she did not open her lips in remonstrance.

With a quiet smile, Mr. Fielding said: "You have not yet heard the tidings with regard to our little friend here, I presume?"

"Tidings—what?" The schoolmaster looked hastily round and saw Kate's head droop, and a twinkle come in the rector's eye. A slight flush rose to his temples.

"Merely that she has received an offer"—

"Offer?" Bramber caught his breath, and the colour left his face.

"Of marriage," continued Mr. Fielding composedly. "A most remarkable offer. The young man is eminently respectable, very comfortably off; age suitable; looks prepossessing; parents acquiescing."

"Kate! Kitty!" Bramber's voice was sharp with alarm and pain.

"I do not know whether the attachment has been one of long continuance," proceeded the rector. "The fact of the proposal—now passing through Coombe—is like the dropping of a meteorite in its midst. Popular fame had attributed Rose Ash to John Pooke."

"John Pooke, is it?" gasped the schoolmaster, and he sprang to his feet.

"John Pooke the younger, not the father, who is a widower of many years' standing. The disparity of ages makes that quite impossible. The younger John it is who has aspired."

"Kate, tell me—it cannot be. It must not be," exclaimed Bramber, stepping before the girl, and in his excitement catching her hands and drawing them from her face, in which she had hidden them. She looked up at him with a flutter in her eyes and hectic colour in her cheeks. She made no attempt to withdraw her hands.

"By the way," said the rector, "I will look up cockfighting in my *Encyclopædia Britannica,* and make an extract from the article, if I find one, that may be serviceable to you, Bramber, when you call on Mr. Puddicombe. I'll go to my library. I shall not detain you many minutes."

The many minutes were protracted to twenty. When Mr. Fielding returned, the young people were seated close to each other under the mulberry-tree, and still held hands; their eyes were bright, and their cheeks glowing.

"I am sorry I have been so long," said the rector; "but there was a great deal of matter under the head of 'Cockpit' in the *Encyclopædia*; and I had to run through it, and cull what would be of greatest utility. I have written it out. Do not rise. I will sit beside you—no, not between you—listen! 'It must appear astonishing to every reflecting mind, that a mode of diversion so cruel and inhuman as that of cockfighting should so generally prevail, that not only the ancients, barbarians, Greeks, and Romans should have adopted it; but that a practice so savage and heathenish should be continued by Christians of all sorts, and even pursued in these better and more enlightened times.' That is how the article begins—very true, but won't do for Mr. Puddicombe. 'The islanders of Delos, it seems, were great lovers of cockfighting; and Tanagra, a city in Bœotia, the Isle of Rhodes, Chalcis in Eubœa, and the country of Media, were famous for their generous and magnanimous race of chickens.' I don't think this is much good. Puddicombe, though a schoolmaster, will hardly know the whereabouts of Delos, Tanagra, Rhodes, and Chalcis. 'The cock is not only an useful animal, but stately in his figure, and magnificent in his plumage. His tenderness towards his brood is such, that, contrary to the custom of many other males, he will scratch and provide for them with an assiduity almost equal to that of the hen; and his generosity is so great, that, on finding a hoard of meat, he will chuckle the hens together, and, without touching one bit himself, will relinquish the whole of it to them. He was called *the bird,* κατ' ἐξοχήν by many of the ancients'—But, bless me, are you attending?"

"Mr. Fielding," answered Bramber, "I do not think I shall have much trouble in finding a topic on which to speak with my predecessor in the school. He was Kitty's schoolmaster. She will introduce me to him. We will go to him at once; and when he hears what we have to say,—that I, the new schoolmaster, am going to take to me the favourite, most docile, the best scholar of the old one; and when he learns that he is the first person to whom we make the announcement, and that he is at liberty to run up and down, and in and out of every house, communicating the news,—why, I am pretty sure that he will be won."

"Well, now!"

"And Kitty will cease to be Kitty Alone some time next year."

CHAPTER XXXI

ON MISCHIEF BENT

When Pasco returned from Newton, he drew up his tax-cart close to the door of the storehouse, took the horse out, but did not unharness him; he merely removed the bridle and gave the brute a feed.

Then he entered the dwelling-house and seated himself at the kitchen table without a word to his wife, and emptied his pocket on the board. A couple of sovereigns and a few shillings clinked together. With his forefinger he separated the gold from the silver coins.

"What! money come in, in place of going out?" asked Zerah. Then, looking over his shoulder, she said, "And precious little it is."

"Little is better than nothing," growled Pasco. "I got this from Cole, the baker. I'd somehow forgot he owed me a trifle, and he stopped me and paid his account. I owe something to the miller, so I'm no better off than I was. In at one pocket, out at the other."

"Now look here, Pasco," said his wife. "For first and last I say this. I have laid by a trifle that I have earned by cockles and winkles, whilst you have been chucking away in coals and wool. If you will pass me your word not to run into extravagance, and not to listen to any more of Jason's schemes, I will let you have this. No"—she corrected her intent; "you are not to be trusted with the money. It shall not leave my hand to go into yours. And your word ain't of any strength, it is as weak as your resolutions. I'll settle the matter of the coals with the merchant at Teignmouth; that is the great call at this moment. I don't do it for you, but to avoid the scandal of having bailiffs in the house—a house where I've kept myself respectable so many years, and where my Wilmot was born and died. I wouldn't have the brokers sell the bed she laid on when dead, not for all my savings. So I'll over to Teignmouth and see what I can manage about the coal merchant's bill; and you, just take that money and pay Ash the miller, and have done with him."

Again the thought rose up in the mind of Pasco that the Evil One was making sport of him. At one time he was in a condition of hopelessness, in another moment there was a lightening in the sky before him. The means of striking fire had been put into his hands at the same time that he was shown that his difficulties were not insurmountable. But the heart which has once resolved on a crime very speedily comes to regard this object as a goal at which it must necessarily aim, and to look with impatience upon all suggestions of relief, upon all dissuasives, and stubbornly, with shut eyes, to pursue the course determined on. The struggle to form the determination once overpassed, the mind shrinks from entering into struggle again, and allows itself to be swept along as though impelled by fatality, as though launched on a stream it is powerless to oppose.

Now his wife's suggestion that she should go to Teignmouth and settle with the merchant for the coals opened up to him a prospect, not of relief from his pecuniary difficulty, but of getting rid of her to enable him the more easily to carry out his intention unobserved. He put his shaking hand into his breast-pocket for his handkerchief, and in pulling this forth drew out also the lucifer match-box, that in falling rattled on the table.

"What have you there, Pasco?" asked Zerah.

"Nothing," he answered, and hastily replaced the box.

"Don't tell me that was nothing which I saw and heard," said his wife testily.

"Well—it's lozenges."

"Didn't know you had a cough."

"Never mind about that, Zerah," said Pasco. "If you go to Teignmouth it must be at once, or the tide will be out, and I don't see how you can get back to-night."

"I've my cousin, Dorothy Bray, there. I'll go to her. I've not seen her some months, and she has a room. I'll leave Kitty at home now, to attend to the house, and you won't need me to the morning flow. I suppose, between you, you can manage to light a fire?"

Pasco started and looked at his wife with alarm, thinking that she had read his thoughts; but he was reassured by her changing the topic "There—I'll give you three pounds towards the miller's bill."

Pepperill was now all anxiety to hurry his wife off. He urged precipitancy on account of the falling tide. He bade her row herself across, and leave the boat on the farther shore till the next morning.

His impatience in a measure woke her suspicion.

"You seem mighty eager to get rid of me," she said querulously.

"'Tain't that, Zerah," he answered; "but I want myself to be off to Brimpts."

"To Brimpts?—and leave Kitty alone in the house?"

"No; I shall take her with me."

"What!—leave the house to take care of itself?"

"What can harm it? No one will break in. They know pretty well there is nothing to be got but bills that ain't paid."

"I don't half like it—and the stores?"

"There is no moving wool or coals without waggons, and I shall lock up."

Zerah stood in uncertainty.

"I wish you'd not go, Pasco."

"I may or may not—but be off, or you'll get stuck in the mud, as did Kitty."

In ten minutes Pasco was alone. He stood on the platform where were the tea-tables and benches, and watched till his wife was half-way across. Then he drew a long breath, and passed through the house, went out at the main door, and hastened to the cart. Again he stood still, and looked searchingly in every direction; then he let down the flap behind, drew out first the sack of shavings and carried it within, and then he cleared out all that remained. He was not satisfied till with a broom he had swept every particle of chip within, leaving not a tell-tale white atom without. Then he tacked some scraps of sacking over the window that no one might look within, and he proceeded to place bundles of the shavings among the coals, not in one great heap, but dispersed in handfuls here and there, and he broke up some pieces of board into splinters and thrust them among the shavings.

He was startled by a voice calling in the door, "Uncle, are you here?"

Hot, agitated, and alarmed, Pasco hastened to the entrance, and saw Kate.

"What do you want? Why are you shouting?"

"Where is aunt? I want to see her. I cannot find her in the house. I have something to tell her."

"You are not like to find her," said Pepperill, coming outside and locking the door behind him. "She is gone over the water, and will stay at Cousin Bray's; and I'm off to Brimpts again, and mean to take you."

"Why, uncle! we have but just returned from there."

"Well, that's no concern of yours, where you are, so long as you have your eatin' and drinkin'. I must go, and your aunt thinks I mustn't leave you alone. So be sharp; run and put what things you require together, and I will harness the cob."

"How long shall we be away, uncle?"

"We shall be back to-morrow evening, or the day after. I can't say. Come, be quick. I can't wait talking with you; it is late already."

Kate obeyed, a little surprised. She speedily returned, with her little bundle tied up in a scarlet kerchief.

Pasco was ready and waiting. He was looking up at the drift of the clouds. The wind was from the east and blowing strongly.

Pepperill drove through the village. He halted at the public-house to call out the taverner, ask for a glass of ale, and tell him he was bound for Dartmoor. At the mill he again drew up, and shouted for the miller, who, on emerging from his door, saluted Pasco with the remark, "Why, you are on the road to-day a great deal. I thought you had gone this way already."

"So I had—to Newton; but there I learned something. The Government has come round to a reasonable mind, and will buy my timber. Not at Devonport, but at Portsmouth; and I am going to measure up. I ran home to tell my old woman. And now, by the way, I will settle that little account between us, if agreeable to you."

"Always right with me to receive," said the miller.

Pasco drew out a handful of money and discharged his debt. "Just receipt it, will you, with the date, and say what o'clock in the afternoon also—that there may be no mistake."

"You are not going to Brimpts to-night?"

"Yes, I am. Business must be attended to."

"Rather late for the little maid by the time you get there."

"That can't be helped—she is strong now."

Then Pepperill drove on. He continued his course without interruption, as the country he passed through was sparsely populated.

Kate's heart was full. She was in doubt whether to tell her uncle that which had taken place between herself and Walter Bramber. She would greatly have preferred to have made the communication to her aunt and let her inform Mr. Pepperill. She was afraid of Pasco. He was violent and brutal. Her aunt was merely harsh. Pasco had been very angry with her for refusing Jan Pooke, and she did not believe that he would receive with favour the communication she had to make relative to the schoolmaster. She dreaded another outburst. Yet her strong sense of duty pressed her to communicate to him what he must learn within a short time, from other lips if not from her own. Then ensued a painful struggle in her breast, and she was constrained to free herself at length, and to say—

"Uncle, you know I refused Jan Pooke, but since then, what I could not say to him I have said to Walter Bramber, the schoolmaster."

"Oh, ah! Jan Pooke—yes, to be sure."

"No, not Jan, but the schoolmaster."

"Drat it!" exclaimed Pasco, stroking his head; "I've forgotten to lock up the house. I let the door stand as it was when you came out. Now anyone can go in and take what they like, break into my bureau and steal my money, get hold of Zerah's silver spoons. I say, Kitty, jump out and open that field-gate. There is a linhay there. I'll put up the trap and horse, and you shall wait by 'em whilst I run back to Coombe Cellars and lock the house."

"But how is aunt to get in when she returns?"

"You be easy. I'll put the key in the little hole over the lintel. She knows where to find it. Look alive, jump and open the gate. Drat it! what a way I shall have to run!"

"Why not drive back, uncle?"

"Why not?—Because the cob must be spared. I've been into Newton already to-day, and the distance he has to go is just about enough to rub his hoofs down."

Pepperill drove the cart into the field indicated, whilst Kate held wide the gate. Then he took the cob out and ran the cart under cover.

"You keep in shelter, and mind you do not show yourself. If anyone pass along the road, be still as a mouse. Never mind who it may be. I shall be gone perhaps an hour, perhaps a little more. It will be dark before I am back. You keep close. There is some straw in the corner, lie on that and go to sleep. We have still a long journey to take, and get on we must, through the night, and this is a darned matter detaining me. Hush!"

They heard something like a cart rattling along.

"Git along, Neddy! 'If I had a donkey 'wot wouldn't go'—you know the rest, Neddy."

"It is my father, I believe," said Kate.

"I don't believe it is. Anyhow, be still," whispered Pasco. "Your father is at Brimpts. He can't be returned here. It's some other chap with a donkey."

The sound of the wheels was lost, as at the point where they had turned in at the gate there was a sweep in the road between high hedges and overarching trees.

"I think it was father," said Kate.

"And I say it was not. However, whoever it was, he's gone now. You bide here. I'm off—mind don't be seen or heard by nobody till my return."

Then Pasco departed.

He did not take the way by the road. He crossed the field, scrambled over a hedge, and directed his course towards the river. This was not the shortest way, and it was certainly the most arduous, for it entailed the breaking through of several hedges, and the scrambling over many banks.

The evening was rapidly closing in.

He saw—or heard—the keeper, and crouched under a hedge, holding his breath. Happily for him, the man passed at some distance. His dog barked, but was called to heel, and Pasco did not venture from his lurking-place till ten minutes after the man had gone his way. Then he sprang up and ran, and did not relax his pace till he had reached the river bank, having first floundered through a backwater deep in mire. On the bank was a foot-path, somewhat frequented by lovers at dusk, and Pasco advanced along it stealthily, listening and peering before him at intervals, to make certain that no one approached.

The tide was out, the mud exhaled its peculiar and not pleasant odour. Something flopped into it near at hand—whether a bird had dropped, or a stone had been flung, or a flounder had been left by the tide, and beat the mud with his tail, Pasco could not tell. The sound sent the blood with a rush to his heart and turned him sick and giddy.

Looking at him over a rail was a white horse. He did not see it until close upon the bank, and then the apparition of the great head turning to him and rubbing its chin on the rail gave him another start, and he almost slipped into the mud beside the path.

At length he reached the field adjoining the spit of land on which stood Coombe Cellars; here the path turned towards the village, but there was a way through the hedge to his own house. Pasco took this track, emerged in front of the Cellars, and found the door open, a light shining through the window of his kitchen and Jason Quarm inside.

CHAPTER XXXII

JASON IN THE WAY

Jason had lighted a candle, and had made himself comfortable in the settle. Pepperill stood staring at him in speechless anger and uncertainty.

"Where's the sister? Where's Kitty?" asked Jason in unconcern.

"What are you doing here?" roared Pasco, convulsed with sudden rage. "Is this your house, that you dare come in and use it as your home?"

Quarm looked at his brother-in-law in surprise.

"Get out of the place at once," shouted Pasco. "If I happen to go away for ten minutes, is that a reason for every Jack and Tom to come here, as if it was 'Beggars' Hall'?"

"Why, what on earth has put you out?"

"What has put me out? you—by coming in here. This is my house, not yours."

"Brother-in-law," said Jason, puzzled at the strange humour of Pasco, "is not that a sufficient answer, when I give you that title? Zerah is my sister—I have ever been welcome here. Kate is my daughter—she lives with you. Why am I here? Put it—I have come to see my sister, come to kiss my child."

"Neither is in the house."

"Then where are they?"

"I am not bound to answer you," shouted Pepperill in anger, vexation, and fear, aggravated by the coolness with which Quarm answered him.

"Yes, you are. I have ties of blood, and ties of affection, your bad temper can't snap. I ask, where is my daughter?"

"Gone back to the moor."

"That can't be—alone."

"She is not alone."

"Is Zerah with her?"

"No, she is not; Zerah is at Teignmouth, gone there to get me out of one of the difficulties into which you have plunged me."

"I—I got you into difficulties? I am always showing you rope's-ends by which you may crawl out."

"Who else but yourself has now put me in such an upsetment that I do not know under what stone to look for money; that I'm threatened with legal proceedings; that the bailiffs are on the way to my house?"

"It is your own doing, not mine. Who threatens you?"

"There is my bill for the wool unmet. There is my account for coals unpaid."

"I have had to do with neither. You acted like a fool about Coaker's wool—buying when in all the papers it was told how that there had been an importation from New South Wales."

"I never read the papers."

"Then you have no right to do business. You do it at inevitable loss. But this is neither here nor there, above nor below. Where is Kate?"

"I have told you—gone to the moor."

"When?"

"An hour or two ago."

"With whom?"

"With me."

"Then how came you here?"

"Because I had left the doors unlocked against impertinent fellows coming in. I left Kate with the trap whilst I ran back. Now, are you content? Out of my house immediately. I want to lock up and go back to her."

"This is a queer tale," said Quarm. "I have myself but just arrived. I must have passed you on the way."

"Not at all, if we had gone into a friend's for a cup of tea."

"With what friends were you?"

"I shall not stand and be catechised by you. I say, get out. I am going to lock up."

"Now look here, Pasco, and be reasonable. I would not have returned to Coombe and left the men at Dart-meet unlooked after, had I not good news to communicate."

"Good news?" mocked Pepperill. "The best of news would be that you were going to take yourself off."

"I believe we shall sell the oak."

"I have heard of that already—from Coaker."

"Well, I tell you it is so. The authorities at Portsmouth will take it at a reasonable price, if we deliver it."

"There is the thing we can't do—that spoils it all."

"Yes, we can—deliver it here in the Teign. There is the Stover Canal—we can send it down by that and ship it all to Portsmouth right away."

Pepperill was silent. This was indeed a rift in the cloud. "The only difficulty is not this—it is that we must have the timber sawn at Brimpts, and sent down and put on board in planks. They cannot freight a vessel with rude oak timber unsawn. Now I have a scheme—there is the river Dart pouring down its volumes of water of no good to anyone. Let us put up a saw-mill, and we shall have the oak run into planks and ready for transport in a jiffy."

"And the cost?"

"Forty pounds."

"Forty pounds?" roared Pasco, and thrust Quarm from him by a rude stroke on the shoulder. "Where am I to look for forty pence?"

"It is our only chance. I must agree to-morrow, or the thing is off. If I engage to saw up the timber and despatch it by water, we shall get a very tidy profit—not what we had hoped, but something. If I do not accept the offer, then I really do not see my way to disposing of the oak at all. The felling of the Okehampton Park oaks has spoiled the market in this country. Come, what say you, Pasco—shall I settle?"

"I cannot do it," answered Pepperill, a cold sweat breaking out over his brow.

"There is an old mine wheel available. I can buy it for a song," said Quarm.

"I have no money. Have I not told you that—or must I knock it into your brain with my fist—or the house key?" He raised his hand threateningly.

"Be reasonable, Pasco. I cannot tell what has come over you to-night. You are not yourself. If you do not care about the outlay for a saw-mill, we must saw all up by hand, and that will come costlier in the end. I fancy if you bestirred yourself you could raise a loan."

"I will not. I will have but one thing now—your absence. Get out of my house!"

"Where be I to go to?" asked Quarm, settling himself from one leg to the other. "There's Jane Redmore in my cottage, with all her children."

"Well"—

"I can't go there—the place is full."

"You are a fool to have suffered it."

"Kate begged and prayed of me"—

"Take the consequences, and be homeless."

"I cannot, for to-night. You are going to Brimpts, and it is as well the men should see you. I shall return to-morrow, but to-night I must house me somewhere. Let me stay here; there is no one in the place, and I'll keep guard for you if you wish."

"There is nothing here to guard, but emptiness. I want no help of yourn."

"But I must have a roof over my head at night."

"Any roof but mine. Will you go, or must I fling you out and down the steps?"

"You're in a wonderful queer temper to-night. What is up?"

"My temper, as you say, is up; and like to be so—when it is through you I am brought to ruin and beggary."

He caught Jason by the shoulders, whirled him round, and with hands and knees thrust him out of the door, and then he slammed it behind him and turned the key. Next moment he blew out the light. Then he threw himself panting on the settle and buried his head in his hands.

He had not sat there many minutes before Quarm was kicking at the door, and calling him by name. Transported with anger, Pasco sprang to his feet, took down the blunderbuss that was over the kitchen fire, and, going to the door, half opened it and thrust forth the muzzle of his piece.

"Go away, or I will shoot."

"This is rank folly!" bawled Jason. "Are you gone demented? Give me shelter for the night; I will do no harm. What do you mean by refusing me such a reasonable request? I tell you I can't go home—all the Redmores are there packing every corner."

Jason thrust up the end of the blunderbuss, and put his shoulder to the door.

"I'll kill you if you trouble me further," said Pasco between his teeth. "Take the consequences of befriending scoundrels and their families."

He drove Quarm back and refastened the door, then he stood at the door listening, with the butt of the gun on his foot. He heard his brother-in-law growl and pass remarks upon him. He heard him limp away, and then all was still.

Pepperill stepped to a window and looked out, to observe the direction taken by Quarm, but the darkness was too great for him to see anything. He went back to the settle and tried to think.

The elaborate precautions he had taken to dissemble his return, to make believe that he had departed before sunset, had been made futile by the appearance of Jason on the scene. Should what he purposed take place—then he could not declare that he had been from home at the time. What availed it that he had paid the miller's bill at a quarter to seven, when his brother-in-law could aver that he had been back at the Cellars an hour later?

What was to be done? Should he abandon his intention because of this mischance? Rage against his brother-in-law ate into his heart. All had promised so well. Everything was moving with such smoothness, till Quarm appeared. What but a malevolent mind could have brought this fellow back from Brimpts to cross him?

What was to be done? It was of no practical use storming against Jason. Should he abandon his purpose or defer it?

To abandon it seemed to him an impossibility. By carrying it out alone could he be released from his present pecuniary difficulty. To defer it was difficult, for he wanted immediate relief; moreover, when again could he calculate on having the ground so clear now—his wife as away in Teignmouth, his niece waiting at a distance with the cart?

What if Jason had seen him? Would he dare to give evidence against him—his own brother-in-law? Was it not to Jason's interest that he, Pasco, should be flush of money, and ready to embark in the proposed scheme of erecting a saw-mill?

Even if Jason spoke of having seen him, he could deny it. Pasco sprang from the settle. He would run the risk. It was worth it.

CHAPTER XXXIII

ONE CRIME LEADS TO ANOTHER

Pasco remained in the dark in his house for about half an hour, waiting till he supposed that Jason was far away. He allowed him time to harness his ass, put it into the cart, and depart. He went once or twice to the door to listen, but did not venture to open it, lest Jason should be without, and should take advantage of the occasion to burst in. He remained all the while bathed in a clammy sweat, his hair stuck to his skull as though plastered about his temples with fish-glue, he felt it heavy and dank on his head like a cap.

Repeatedly did he try to collect his thoughts and to coolly consider whether it were not advisable for him, under the circumstances, to abandon his scheme. But his thoughts were in a condition of dislocation, he could not gather them and fit them together into consecutive order. He felt himself impelled, having formed his resolve, to proceed with it, and to leave to the future the removal of such difficulties as might spring up, as came in his way.

He was restless, yet afraid to be stirring. He was impatient for the time to pass, and counted the ticks of the clock, yet forgot after a few minutes the number he had reached.

The seat was hard and bruised him, he leaned back, and his back ached. He held out his hand, placed it on the table and endeavoured to steady it. He was aware that it shook, and he used all the power of his will to arrest its convulsive quiver, but ineffectually. At length, unable longer to endure inaction, and convinced that sufficient time had elapsed for his brother-in-law to have got away, he cautiously unlocked the door and looked out.

In the dark he could see no one; he listened and could hear no sound.

Then he stepped back to the kitchen table and removed the candle-end from the stick, and put it into his pocket. No sooner had he reached the door again, however, than it occurred to him that a candlestick without a tallow candle in it, if left on the table, would attract attention and comment. He therefore returned for it, and placed it on the mantelshelf above the hearth. In doing this he knocked over a canister that fell at his feet. He groped and found the canister; the cover had come off, and some of the contents were spilled. This was gunpowder. Greatly disconcerted, Pasco felt for a brush and swept all the grains he could into the hollow of his hand, and shook them into his trousers-pocket, then he swept the brush vigorously about, so as to disperse over the floor any particles that had escaped him in the dark. After which he proceeded carefully to replace the canister. He now again made his way to the door, passed without, locked the door behind him, and placed the key in a hollow above the lintel, known to Zerah and himself.

Then he stealthily crossed the yard to his great warehouse, but at every second step turned his ears about, listening for a sound which might alarm him.

He did not breathe freely till he was within his store. He had not locked it—indeed, of late he had been wont to leave it unfastened, labouring under the hope that the hint thrown out to Roger Redmore might be taken by the fellow, thus relieving himself of his self-imposed task.

Without, there was a little light from the grey sky. Within was none. What amount might have found its way in through the window was excluded by the sacking that Pasco had nailed over the opening.

He now proceeded to light his candle end. When the wick was kindled, he looked about him timidly, then with more confidence; lastly with a sensation of great regret and even pity for the fabric in which he had so long stored his supplies that he retailed to the neighbourhood.

But no thought of retreat came over his mind now, he was impelled forward irresistibly. The doubt was past that had tortured him, after his interview with Jason Quarm.

He stuck the candle-end upon the ground, and went about among the coals, examining the places where he had put the shavings, adding here and there some bits of stick, or rearranging the coals, and then strewing over them the contents of his out-turned pocket. Then he sat down and panted. He must rest a moment and wipe his brow before the irrevocable act was accomplished.

Presently, slowly, painfully, he rose from the block of coal on which he had seated himself. The sack lay hard by into which he had stuffed the shavings. It was now empty.

He took up the candle-end and went towards the nearest mass of shavings, stooped—the grease ran over his fingers. The wick had become long and the flame burnt dull. He thought to snuff it with his fingers, but they shook too much to be trusted. He might extinguish the flame, and he shuddered at the thought of being left there—in his old storehouse—in the dark. He again set down the candle, and with a bit of stick beat the red wick, and struck off sparks from it, till he had somewhat reduced the length of the snuff.

He was about to take up the candle to apply it to the shavings, when he heard a sound—a strange grating, rattling sound behind him.

He looked round, but could see nothing, his great body was between the light and the rear of the shed, whence the sound proceeded. He was too much alarmed to perceive the cause of the obscurity. Then he heard a voice—

"Pasco, I never thought you a scoundrel till now—but now I know it."

Pepperill recognised the voice at once—it was that of Jason Quarm.

Immediately he realised the situation. Expelled from Coombe Cellars, debarred from sheltering in his own house, Quarm had entered the store-shed, and had climbed the ladder into the loft to lie among the wool, and there sleep.

A sudden wild, fierce thought shot through Pasco's brain like the flash of summer lightning. He sprang to his feet. The terror that had momentarily unnerved him passed away. Leaving the candle burning on the ground, without a word, he strode to the ladder, which Quarm was descending laboriously, owing to his lameness.

With clenched teeth and contracted brow, and with every muscle knotted like cord, Pepperill threw himself on the ladder, just as Jason got his head below the opening of the loft, and shook it.

"For Heaven's sake! what are you about?" screamed Jason.

"I'll rid myself of a danger," answered Pasco between his teeth and lips, indistinctly, and he twisted the ladder, and kicked at its feet to throw it down.

"Pasco, let go! Pasco, will you kill me?" shrieked the crippled man, catching ineffectually at the floor through which he had crawled, then clutching the side of the ladder.

Pepperill uttered an oath; he ran under the ladder, set his back against it and kicked with his heels.

"Pasco! I'll not tell—I swear!"

"I won't give you the chance," gasped Pepperill. The ladder was reeling, sliding, the feet were slipping on the slate floor. A piercing scream, and down came ladder and man upon Pasco, throwing him on his knees, but precipitating the unfortunate cripple with a crash on the pavement.

Pepperill, though shaken and bruised, was not seriously hurt. He gathered himself up, stretched his limbs, felt his arms, and with lowering brow stepped towards his prostrate brother-in-law, who lay on his back, his arms extended, the hands convulsively contracted. His chin was up, and the dim glow of the candle cast its light below the chin, and had no rays for the upper portion of the face.

Pepperill felt in his pocket for the lucifer matches, and, stooping over Quarm, lit one, and passed the flame over his countenance. Jason was apparently insensible. Blood was flowing from his mouth at the corners. The flame of the match was reflected in the white of the upturned eyes.

Pasco held the match till it burnt his fingers, then he let it fall, and remained considering for a moment. Should he let his brother-in-law lie where he was? Could he be sure that he would not awake from a momentary daze caused by the blow on his head as he fell on the stone floor?

Pasco picked up a huge lump of coal and stood over Jason, ready to dash it down on his head, and make sure of his not awaking. But though his heart was hard, and he was launched on a course of crime, yet conscience makes strange distinctions in crime, and shrinks from doing boldly the evil at which it aims covertly.

Pasco laid aside the block of coal. He would not dash out his brother-in-law's brains, but he would by other means make sure that he should not rouse to give him future trouble.

He took the sack, in which had been the shavings, and proceeded to thrust into it the legs of Quarm, who offered no more resistance than would a dead man, and gave no sign of consciousness. With much labour, Pasco drew the sack up, enclosing the body; he pulled down the arms and forced them into the sack also. But he was unable to envelop Jason completely. The sack was not of sufficient length for the purpose. It reached to his breast and elbows only.

There was a rope hanging in the store to a crook in the wall. Pepperill disengaged this, and with the cord bound Jason's feet, then tightly strapped him about the arms so as to make it impossible for him to free himself, should he return to consciousness.

The exertion used by Pasco had steadied his nerves. He no longer trembled. His hand had ceased to shake, and his heart no longer contracted with fear.

Greatly heated by his labour, he stood up and wiped his brow with his sleeve. Then he was aware of a cool current of air wafting across him, and he saw that in this same current the candle-flame consumed its wick and swaled away profusely. He turned in the direction of the draught, and found that the door into the shed was partly open. He had not locked it when he entered, but had closed it. The night wind had swung it ajar, and then by its own weight it had opened farther. Pepperill shut it again, and placed a lump of coal against the foot to prevent a recurrence of the same thing.

As he returned to where Jason lay, he heard a slight noise overhead, and saw a white and black pigeon perched on a swinging pole.

The bird was young. It had been given to Pasco the week before, as he had expressed a wish to have pigeons. He had shut the bird up in his shed to accustom it to regard the shed as its home, and to remain there. He had fed the bird himself with crumbs, and had entertained an affection for it.

Now a qualm came over his heart. He could not bear to think of this innocent bird falling a victim. He had compunction for the pigeon, none for the unconscious Jason. Therefore, rolling a barrel under the perch, he climbed upon it, captured the sleep-stupid bird and carried it between his hands to the door, pushed aside the lump of coal, and threw the pigeon into the open air without.

That act of mercy accomplished, he shut the door and went back to where the candle was. This he now detached from the floor and the mass of melted tallow around it, and applied the flame to one, then to another, of the little parcels of combustibles in various places. Flames danced about, and for a minute Pasco looked on with satisfaction, assuring himself that the shavings had ignited the sticks, and the sticks had kindled the coals. When well satisfied that all was as he desired, he knelt down, and by sheer force rolled the heavy, lifeless body of Jason Quarm from the floor, up the slope of the coals, and lodged it among large blocks on the top.

Then Pepperill turned, extinguished his candle, went out through the door, locked it, and started at a run across the fields in the direction whence he had come an hour before.

CHAPTER XXXIV

AND YET ANOTHER

Pasco ran on, easily surmounting the hedges which he had clambered over with difficulty on his way to Coombe Cellars. He reached the track by the water's edge, and ran along that without once looking behind him, and only paused when he arrived at the point at which he must strike inland, to his left, leaving the river margin to ascend the sloping shaws in the direction of the shed where tarried Kitty with cob and cart. Here he halted, and a chill ran through his arteries, making him shiver and his teeth chatter. He was hot with running, yet withal in an icy tremor, and with a feeling of swimming in his head and sickness at his heart.

The thought had risen up in him, an almost tangible thought, like a great beast coiled in his heart, stretching itself, getting on its feet, and turning. The thought was this—that it was not too late to save his brother-in-law. He might return, unlock the store, rush in, and drag the unconscious man down from the heap of coals, through the smoke and flame. The fire had not yet reached him; it was tonguing up the heap, sending the tips of its flames tastingly towards him; the fire was hot beneath, but the crust still upheld the man in the sack; would it be so much longer? As the coals were consumed beneath, there would be formed a great core of red fire, and if Jason moved, the crust would give way, and then, shrieking, unable to assist himself, he would drop into that glowing mass, where the cords would be burnt to free him, but only when it would be too late for him to escape.

Had Jason already woke from his trance, and was he cuddled up in his sack, watching the approaching flames, crying for help, and getting none? Was he tearing at his bands with his teeth, writhing—trying to precipitate himself down the black mound of combustible material, in the hopes of being able to roll along the floor to the door? And if he succeeded so far—what more could he do? Nothing but watch the fire grow, break out in gushes of scarlet and orange, pour forth volumes of stifling smoke, and then lie with his mouth below the door, gasping for the air that rushed in beneath.

Shuddering, Pasco Pepperill stood with eyes open, looking into the night, seeing all this as really as though the vision were unrolled before his naked eyes. He dared not look behind him, his neck was stiff, and he could not turn it—he could not even turn his eyes in the direction of the Cellars.

Should he retrace his course and free Jason? Could he not rely on Jason to remain silent after this terrible experience? But what if he arrived too late? What if the fire had already broken out, and had laid hold of its prey? Why should he give himself the lasting horror of seeing what he must then see? And of what avail would it be to the burning man?

It was too late. Pasco had taken his line, had cast his lot, and there was no return. He resumed his run up the hill, through the meadows; the wind blowing off the river assisted him. When he reached the field in which was the shed, he knew that Coombe Cellars was no longer visible. There was a shoulder of hill between.

But though the Cellars might not be visible, the sky overhead might show redness, might throb with light; and lest he should see this, he fixed his eyes resolutely in an opposite direction.

In crossing the field he no longer ran. He had lost his breath ascending the hill; he walked slowly, panting, and ever and anon stopped to wipe his brow, and remove his hat, that the cool wind might play about his wet hair.

The qualm of conscience relative to Jason was overpassed, and now Pepperill congratulated himself on his success. Now—all was as could be desired, there was nothing to inculpate him, no one to turn evidence against him, except—

There was one person, and one only, who was a danger to Pasco; one person, and one only, who knew that he had been to Coombe Cellars after having ostensibly left it; one, and one only, that he had been on the spot precisely at the time when, presumably, the fire broke out.

If Kate Quarm were to speak, then what he had done was done in vain; the Company would refuse to pay the sum for which his stock was insured, and he might be suspected of having caused the death of his brother-in-law. Would not Kate speak—when she knew that her father was dead? Might she not make dangerous admissions should there be an inquest? The charred corpse or burnt bones would be discovered when the ashes of the store were removed, and Jason's cart and ass being in Coombe, would lead to the conclusion that he, Jason Quarm, had caused the conflagration and had perished in it. It would be supposed that he had gone to the Cellars, and, finding it locked and no one within, had taken shelter for the night in the warehouse, where he had lit his pipe, gone to sleep, and inadvertently had set fire to the coals and wool.

But then—what might Kate be brought to say if questioned by the coroner?

Pepperill entered the shed and called the girl. He called twice before he received an answer. Then he struck a light, and as the match flared he saw before him the drowsy face of Kate.

"Oh, uncle! What a long time you have been away! I fell asleep."

"Long time? I have not been a quarter of an hour. I ran to the Cellars and ran back the whole way."

"It has been more than a quarter of an hour, Uncle Pasco. I waited, watching for ever such a time, and then I went to sleep."

"You are mistaken. Because you shut your eyes you think the time was long."

"What is that, uncle, you are burning?"

"A lucifer match."

"How did you get it alight?"

"By striking it on the box."

"How could that light it? Is there a bit of tiny flint on the match and steel on the box?

"No, there is not. I don't know how the fire comes—but it comes somehow."

"That must be a very curious contrivance, uncle."

"Whether curious or not is no concern of yours."

He struck another match and held it aloft. The girl stood on one side of the cart, he on the other. The lucifer flame twinkled in her eyes. Her hair was ruffled with sleep.

As Pasco looked at her by the dying flame, he was considering what to do. He had no doubt that he was insecure so long as she lived. Desperate, hardened, projected along an evil course, could he withhold his hand now and not make himself secure? Would it not be weakness as well as folly to allow this testimony to remain who could at any moment reveal his guilt? But if he were to strike her down with a stake or stone, what could he do with the body?

"Take care, uncle," said Kate. "There is dry furze here. If the spark falls, there may be a blaze."

He extinguished the match with his fingers. He did not desire that his course should be marked by fires.

"Is there much furze here, Kitty?" he asked in a smothered voice.

"Oh no! only just under foot."

"No great heap in a corner?"

"None, uncle."

"Not enough to cover you over if you were asleep."

Kate laughed and answered, "I would never lie on furze if I could help it, and be covered with it—I should be tormented with prickles. I sat down and laid my head against the hedge that makes the back of the linhay." He was prodding the bedding of furze with his whip. "It is all fresh," said Kate. "I reckon Miller Ash is going to turn his cow in here, when he has taken away her calf."

"Ah! she has calved?"

"Yes; last week."

"True—the cow will be here to-morrow, or in a couple of days." To himself he muttered, "It won't do"—then aloud, "Jump into the cart, Kitty. We must push on. You drive out, I will open the gate."

In another minute Pasco Pepperill was in his seat with Kitty at his side, driving in the direction away from the Cellars.

He feared every moment to hear her say, "Uncle, what is that light shining over Coombe? Can there be a fire?"

Instead of that she said, "Uncle, did you see nothing of my father? I am quite sure that was he who drove by after we had got into Mr. Ash's field. I heard his voice. I know his way with the donkey. I am quite certain that was father."

"Your father?—no. Never set eyes on him. You were mistaken."

"I am sure it was my father. I know the rattle of the cart wheel."

"I say it was not; and take care how you say a word about ever having gone into the field, and about my having returned to the Cellars."

"Why, uncle?"

"Because Ash will summons me for trespass, and because my horse ate the grass. That's one reason; but there's a better one—I don't choose that you should speak."

Kate was accustomed to his rough manner, and she did not answer.

Then Pasco's mind began to work on the theme that had occupied it before. He had been seen driving out of Coombe with Kate at his side. But what of that? Would it not be a sufficient answer to give, were she not to be seen again, that he had met Jason Quarm on the road, and that the man had taken his daughter with him, and that thereupon both had perished in the flames?

The more he considered the matter, the more essential to his security did it seem to him that Kate should be got rid of. The only embarrassment he felt was as to the means to be employed, and the place where it was to be done. Not till she was removed could the weight now oppressing his mind be cast off.

"Uncle," said Kate after a long course in silence, "I cannot think how that lucifer acts, if there be no flint and no steel. How else can the match be made to light?"

"How is no matter to me—kindle it does, somehow." Then, abruptly, "Have you got your cotton dress on? The wind is from the east and chilly."

"Oh no, uncle, I have on my thick woollen dress, and am very warm—thank you kindly for considering me."

"The thick wool, is it?"

"Yes, uncle—very sure, very thick and warm."

Then that would not do. It had occurred to him to drop a lighted match on her frock, set her in flames, and throw her out into the road at a lonely spot. No, that would not do. He reversed his whip and beat the cob with the handle.

"Diamond is not going badly, uncle," said Kate in mild remonstrance.

He was in reality trying the weight of the whip handle and the stiffness of the stem. That would not effect his purpose; there was no metal to signify at the butt-end. The horse did not greatly mind a blow dealt it with a full swing of its master's arm.

Pasco bore no malice against his niece. In his cold fashion he liked her. She was useful in the house, and saved him the expense of a maid. It was doubtful whether any servant would have been as submissive to Zerah as was Kitty, whether any would have continued so long in service to her. He had forgotten his momentary resentment at Kate refusing the offer of John Pooke. He wished the girl ill for no other reason than his own safety. Had he been able to send her away, out of the country, that would have satisfied him. But as there was no opportunity for getting her out of the way without hurt to himself, she must be removed by such means as were possible to him.

How to do this, and where to do it, remained undecided. Not where he then was could it be attempted, for he was now approaching Newton. The lights were twinkling through the trees, cottages were passed with illumined windows, and sometimes with persons standing in the doors.

On entering Newton, Pepperill turned his horse's head to make a detour, so as to avoid passing the inn that had been rebuilt after having been burnt down. For some reason undefined in his own heart, he shrank from driving before that house.

In a few minutes the cob was trotting along the Ashburton road. Pasco looked behind him. He heard the sound of the hoofs of another horse, and the rattle of other wheels. Some traveller was on the road that night.

"Uncle," said Kate, "I think the moon is going to rise."

"I suppose so."

"Will it not be grand on the moor, with the moon shining over it, and the Dart flowing like silver below?"

"Silver? I wish it were silver, and I'd pocket it," growled Pasco. "Dang it! what is that which is following?"

He slackened his pace, but the conveyance did not pass him; it approached, and the driver was content to keep in the rear.

"Will you go on?" shouted Pasco, turning his head.

"No, we'll remain as we are," answered the driver.

"How far are you going?"

"To Ashburton."

Well, thought Pasco, the loneliest, wildest part of the road is that between Ashburton and Brimpts.

CHAPTER XXXV

UNSUCCESSFUL

On leaving Ashburton, Pasco Pepperill was relieved of the attendance which had been so irksome to him. He would not, probably, have carried out his purpose between Newton and Ashburton, as that was a high road, much frequented, running through cultivated lands, and with farms and cottages along it at no great intervals. Nevertheless, the knowledge irritated him that someone was following him, that should an opportunity otherwise propitious arise, he could not seize it because of the man in the trap at his heels. Never able clearly to bring all contingencies together before his inward eye, in the conduct of his business, he was now more dull and confused in mind than usual.

He took it into his head that there was something menacing in the pursuit; that the man in his rear was aware of what he had done at the Cellars, that he foresaw his present purpose, and was intentionally following him, keeping him in sight, either that he might deliver him up to justice for what he had done, or to prevent the execution of his present design.

It was consequently with immense relief that he heard the man's cheery "Good-night," and his wheels turn off by a by-street, as he trotted through Ashburton and along the road leading to Dart-meet and Brimpts.

At a distance of rather over a mile from Ashburton the Dart is crossed, then the road climbs a steep hill, cutting off the great sweep made by the river as it flows through Holne Chase, and it crosses the river again as it bursts from the moor at Newbridge. Nearly the whole of this way is through woods, and does not pass a single human habitation.

Directly New Bridge is crossed, the character of the surroundings changes. In place of rock and woods of pine and oak and beech, succeed the solitude and desolation of moorland, heather, and furze brake, with at one spot only a cluster of small cottages about a little inn, with a clump of sycamores behind them and a few acres of mountain pasture before them, laboriously cleared of granite boulders. Immediately after passing this hamlet, the road traverses moorland entirely uninhabited. Tors rise to the height of from twelve to fifteen hundred feet; their sides are strewn with rocky ruin. Dense masses of furze cover the moorland sweeps, and between the clefts of the rocks whortleberry grows rankly into veritable bushes, hung in June with purple berries. Below, at the depth of a thousand feet, foams and roars the Dart amidst boulders and bushes of mountain-ash and thorn.

It was obvious to the clouded mind of Pepperill that if he was to get rid of Kitty, it must be done either in the Holne Wood or on the moor. One place was as good as the other for disposal of the child's body; the dense forest growth or the equally dense whortle and furze would effectually conceal it.

When the first Dart bridge was crossed, and the steep ascent begun, Pepperill said roughly to his niece—

"You ain't going to sit here and make the horse drag you all the way up this tremendous hill, be you?"

"No, uncle dear; I was only waiting for you to draw up that I might jump out. Do you see the moon coming up behind the trees, shining through them, like a good thought in the midst of dark imaginings?"

"Dang the moon and your imaginings! Get out."

"I was thinking of something my book says," apologised Kate, descending to the road.

"Your book? What do you mean?"

"I mean that which the schoolmaster gave me, which I have read and read, and in which I always find something new, and always am sure of something true."

"What does the book say?"

"I learned it by heart—

'Within the soul a faculty abides,
That with interpositions'—

That means things which come between. He explained that to me. I cannot always make out what is said till it is explained; but when it is, then the full truth and loveliness rises and shines into me like the moon when it has got over the hills and the woods."

"Go on."

"'A faculty abides,
That with interpositions, which would hide
And darken, so can deal that they become
Contingencies of pomp, and serve to exalt
Her native brightness.'

I did not understand what contingencies meant, but he told me, and now all is quite plain as it is quite true. And it goes on—

'As the ample moon
Rising behind a thick and lofty grove,
Burns like an unconsuming fire, light
In the green trees'"—

"Cease this foolery," said Pasco impatiently. He was fumbling in his pocket for his clasp-knife, and was opening it.

"Do look, uncle dear!" exclaimed Kate, turning to observe the moon as it mounted over the rich Buckland Woods on the farther bank of the Dart.

"Halt," shouted Pasco to the horse.

They had reached an eminence. The girl stood wrapped in delight, with the silver shield of the moon before her, casting its glorious light over her face and folded hands. Pasco had his knife out. She heard the click, as the spring nipped the blade firmly, but did not turn to see what occasioned the sound.

"The moon has come up out of the trees just as he said—I mean the poet—like a power in the heart and soul that has been entangled in all kinds of dark and twisted matters of every day. Oh, uncle, what is that?"

Pasco drew back. A white dog—a mongrel, short-haired lurcher—crossed the road. Simultaneously a whistle was heard, and this was answered by another in the distance.

"There are poachers about," said Pepperill. He shut his knife, pocketed it, and called Kate to get into the trap. He was not going to halt to see a darned moon rise, when all kinds of vagabonds were about, and there was no safety for honest men.

Pasco drove rapidly down the hillside into the Dart Valley at New Bridge. The road was mostly in shadow, but the bare moor on the farther side was white in the moonlight, as though it had been snowed over. The horse was tired, and tripped. Pasco had to be on his guard lest the beast should fall. In the shadow of the trees it could not see the stones that strewed the way. At the bottom of the valley flowed the Dart; the rush of the water breaking over the rocks was audible.

"If a harm came to you or me in the river, I reckon the body would be washed right away to Sharpitor," said Pepperill.

"Uncle!" said Kate, with a laugh, "that would be going up hill."

"I'm getting mazed," growled he; "so it is. Well, folk would say one or other of us had come by an accident among the rocks o' Sharpitor, and tumbled into the river and been carried down by the stream. That's likely—eh?"

"I suppose so, uncle. But if anything were to happen to one, that the other would know, and do all he could to help."

"Of course."

Pepperill was looking at the brawling torrent.

"And if anything were to chance to one here, the body would be carried right down the Chase for miles till it came to the other bridge."

"I daresay, uncle. But don't talk like that. Let us look at the moonlight. There is a man yonder—by the side of the river."

"A man—where?"

"By that large stone."

"He is catching salmon. Not a fish has a chance up here on the moor. What a parcel of rascals there be!"

Pepperill drove across the bridge. He had intended—he hardly dared articulately to express to himself his intention. Again he was frustrated—just at a suitable point—by this fellow catching salmon by night.

Beyond the bridge the road rose rapidly. Both uncle and niece were forced to descend from the cart, and relieve the horse. Some six hundred feet had to be mounted without any zigzags in the road. Kate walked along cheerily. Pasco lagged behind. The horse, with nose down, laboriously stepped up the steep incline. Pasco took out his knife and cut a branch of thorn from the hedge, and in doing so tore his fingers. He put the thorn behind the seat.

When the summit of the hill was almost reached, he said to Kate, "I shall turn to the left, and leave the road."

"What—out on the moor?"

"Yes; I think we can cut off a great curve and avoid the cottages. You walk by the horse's head; I will mount and hold the reins. There are large stones in the way."

This was the case. Kate thought that her uncle was rash in taking the track across the moor at night, a way he could not know, merely to save a mile that the road made in detour. But she said nothing. She was pleased to go by a way that commanded the gorge of the Dart, and had no fear, as the moon shone brilliantly, and every bush and stone was visible as in the day. The mica and spar in the granite made each rock sparkle as though encrusted with diamonds. A heavy dew had fallen, cobwebs hanging on the furze were as silvery fairy tissue.

Rabbits were out sporting, feeding, darting away with a gleam of snowy tail when alarmed. Owls were flitting and hooting in the ravine. The wind from the east hummed an Æolian strain in the moor grass and heather.

The moon rose high above all obstruction to its placid light, and Kate breathed slowly, and in the chill air her breath came away as a fine shining vapour. Every now and then the cob struck out a red fire-spark from the stones against which his shoe struck. Kate held the reins at the bit, and paced at his head, her heart swelling with happiness, as she drank in the loveliness of the night, till she was so full of the beauty that her eyes began to fill. Pasco Pepperill was silent. He was knotting the thorn-branch to his whip. His eye was on her.

Presently the track on the turf ran at the edge of a steep slope. Rocks from a tor overhead had fallen and strewn the incline, and formed fantastic objects in the moonlight, casting shadows even more fantastic. A sheep that had been sleeping under one of the rocks started up and bounded away. The spring of the sheep close beside him alarmed the horse, and he started back, plunged, and dragged Kate off her feet.

Then, with a cry of rage, Pasco rose in the cart, whirled his whip about, and lashed the cob with the full force of his arm, at the same time that he raised the reins in his left and beat with them as well, and jerked at the brute's mouth.

Kate was down. She had slipped; she was before the plunging beast. Pasco saw it. He swore, lashed this side, that, then at the flanks, at the head, at the belly of the tortured brute, that leaped and staggered, kicked and reeled under the strokes of the thorns which tore his skin. He snorted, reared, put down his head; the steam came off him in a cloud.

There was one thing the beast would not do—rush forward and trample on the fallen girl. Pasco saw it, and cursed the horse. He flung himself from the trap, he rushed at the bridle; his foot was on Kate's gown.

"Uncle! uncle!" she cried.

With one hand he dragged the horse forward, with the other he swung the thorn-bush. A step, and the hoofs and wheels of the horse and cart would be over the girl. Then a thrust would suffice to send her down the side of the slope into the torrent below.

But the brute leaped into the air before the swinging thorn-bush, swerved up hill, dragging Pasco at his head, and flung him over a rock. His hand became entangled; he could not for a moment disengage it; he was dragged forward; the head-gear gave way, and Pasco fell among the bushes, crying out with rage and pain. Next moment Kate stood before him.

"What is the matter, uncle dear? Are you hurt? I am safe."

CHAPTER XXXVI

ALL IN VAIN

Pasco Pepperill staggered to his feet, and at once felt pain in one ankle.

"Are you hurt, dear uncle?" again inquired Kate.

"Hurt? I've strained and bruised myself all over. My right arm—my leg—I can hobble only. Where's the trap?"

"If you have no bones broken, uncle, sit down, and I will see after Diamond."

The horse was browsing unconcernedly at no great distance. Too tired to run far, too hungry to heed his wounds, he had at once applied himself to the consumption of the sweet moorland grass. Happily the cart was uninjured. It had not been upset, and no more of the harness was broken than a strap at the head. The cob allowed Kate to approach and take him by the forelock without remonstrance. He knew Kate, who had been accustomed to fondle him, and who, in the absence of friends of her own order, had made one of the brute beast. She managed to fasten up the broken strap and replaced the headstall; then she drew the horse along to where her uncle sat rubbing his leg and arm.

"It's the right arm, drat it!" said Pasco; "won't I only give that cursed beast a leathering when I can use my arm again!"

"Surely, uncle, poor Diamond was going on all right till you beat him. He is so patient that he does not deserve a beating. There is a thorn branch about which the whip has become entangled. I suppose that must have hurt him, poor fellow. He was good, too; when my foot slipped and I fell, he would not trample on me. You were beating him, uncle, and did not see where I was. Just think how good he was!—notwithstanding the thorns, yet he would not tread on me."

"Oh yes, that is all you think about, you selfish minx, your own self. Because you are uninjured, you don't care for me who am bruised all over."

It was of no use pursuing the matter. Kate knew her uncle's unreasonable moods, so she changed the subject and asked, "What is to be done now? shall we go on along the moor or turn back?"

"It is of no use going along the moor now. We may come to some other darned accident with this vile brute. Lead him back along our tracks to the road. I don't want to be thrown out again. This is the second time he has treated me in this manner. If I had a gun, I'd shoot him."

"Uncle, that other occasion was no fault of his. You were driving the schoolmaster, and Walter Bramber told me about it—you sent the wheel against a stone."

"Of course the blame is mine, and this time also. The horse is innocent."

"If you had not beaten poor Diamond"—

"Go on with the cart, and hold your tongue."

But Pasco walked with pain. He had not taken many steps before he asked to be helped up into the trap.

Kate led the horse and spoke caressingly to the brute, that was greatly fagged with the long journey without a break he had taken that evening. Usually he would be given an hour's rest and a feed at Ashburton, before the worst and most arduous portion of the journey was taken; but on this occasion he had been urged on at his fastest pace and never allowed to slacken it, and not given any rest, not even a mouthful of water, at Ashburton. No wonder that he tripped.

Pasco looked sullenly before him at the girl walking in the moonlight, speaking to the horse. The chance of doing her an injury was past. He could with difficulty move his arm. If he drew his knife on her and attacked her there on the moor, she could run from him, and he would be unable to pursue her, owing to his sprained ankle.

There was no help for it, he must make the best of the circumstances, threaten her if she showed an inclination to speak and compromise him. Perhaps, taken all in all, it was as well that his purpose had been frustrated. There was no telling; he might have got into difficulties had he killed her. In escaping from one danger, he might have precipitated himself into another.

He saw now what he had not seen before. It had been his intention to attribute the fire to Jason Quarm. Had Kitty disappeared according to his purpose, then he would have said she had returned to Coombe with her father. It was known that she had left the place in his own company in the trap. She had been seen by the publican and by the miller. But it was possible, it was probable, that Jason had been seen as he drove through Coombe to the Cellars. If so, then it would have been observed that he was alone; accordingly his—Pasco's—story of her return with her father would have been refuted. Then, what explanation could he have given of her disappearance?

Pepperill drew a long breath. He had been preserved from making a fatal mistake. He was glad now that his attempt on Kate had been frustrated.

Then, again, a new idea entered his brain. Could he not have attributed her death to accident on the moor, had the horse trampled on her? He might have done so, but then, would not folks have thought there was something more than coincidence in the death, the same night, of father and daughter?

"I believe I'd ha' been a stoopid if I'd ha' done it," said Pasco, and resigned himself to circumstances. "Be us in the road? I reckon us be."

"Yes, uncle; here is where we turned off from the highway. Which turn shall I take—on to Brimpts or back to Ashburton?"

"On ahead, Brimpts way. There's a little public-house at Pound Gate, and I be that dry, and the cob, I reckon, be that lazy—we'd best turn in there and rest the night. The shaking of the cart hurts me, moreover."

Kate got up into the vehicle and drove. Her uncle gladly resigned the reins to her. He could have held them, indeed, but not have used the whip, and Diamond would not go with him unless he used the whip.

Before long the little tavern was reached—a low building of moorstones, whitewashed, with a thatched roof, and a sign over the door.

To the surprise of Pepperill, he saw a chaise without horses outside.

At the inn he drew up. The landlord came to the door and helped him to descend.

"What! hurt yourself, Mr. Pepperill?"

"Yes; had a spill."

"On your way to Brimpts, I suppose? I hear you are selling the timber."

"Yes, to Government. Have you visitors?"

"Ay! Some one come after you."

"After me?"

Notwithstanding his bad ankle, Pasco started back. Had his face not been in shadow, the landlord might have observed how pale he had become.

"What! come from Coombe?" he asked in a faltering voice.

"Hardly that, master," answered the landlord. "Not likely *that* when you be come from there. No, o' course, came t'other road. He asked about you at Brimpts, and then drove on. He's purposing to sleep the night here, and was intending to push on to Coombe to-morrow. He's ordered some supper, and my old woman ha' done him a couple of rashers and some eggs. Have you a mind to join him?"

"But who is he? What does he want?" Pasco was still uneasy.

"A sort of a lawyer chap."

"A lawyer?" Pepperill hobbled to his trap. "I'll push on, thank ye, I'll not stay."

"Nay, you'd better. I hold wi' you, master, that it is best in general to give clear room to lawyers. But this time I don't think but you'd safest come in. He'll do you no hurt, and maybe he brings you good, Mr. Pepperill."

"I'll go on," said Pasco decidedly. "I hate all lawyers as I do ravens."

"Halloo! What is this?" A gentleman put his head out of the bar parlour window, which was open. "Who is it that hates lawyers? Not Mr. Pepperill?"

Pasco attempted to scramble into his trap.

"Is that Mr. Pepperill, of Coombe Cellars? You must stay. I have a word to speak with you."

"I won't stay—not a minute."

"I'll not charge you six-and-eight. Yet it is something to your advantage. I'm Mr. James Squire, solicitor, Tavistock. I have come about your affairs. Your old uncle, Sampson Blunt, is dead—died of a stroke—sudden—and you come in for everything. What say you now? Will you stay? Will you put up your horse? Will you come in and have some of my rasher and eggs? I'm drinking stout—what will you take? You won't drive any farther to-night, I presume? Sampson has died worth something like three thousand pounds; and every penny comes to you, except what Government claims as pickings—probate duty, you understand."

"Three thousand pounds?" gasped Pasco.

"Ay, not a guinea under, and it may be more. His affairs haven't been properly looked into yet. I came off post-haste, took a chaise from Tavistock, didn't think to meet you. Was coming on to-morrow. An apoplectic stroke. No children, no one else to inherit but yourself, the only heir-at-law. Now, then, what do you say? Rum and milk, they tell me, is the moor tipple, but I go in for stout."

With glazed eyes and open mouth stood Pasco Pepperill, his hands fallen at his side; he seemed as though he had been paralysed.

"Three thousand five hundred—there's no saying," continued Mr. Squire, through the window. "Look sharp, come in, or the rashers and eggs will be cold. I asked for a chop. Couldn't have it. Pleaded for a steak. No good. No butchers on the moor. So ham and eggs, and ham salt as brine. Never mind—drink more. Come in."

Then the head of the lawyer disappeared behind the blind, and the click of his knife and fork was audible.

Pasco tried to raise his right arm, failed, then he clapped his left hand to his brow.

"Good heavens!" he almost shouted; "I've done it all for naught."

"Done what?" asked the innkeeper.

Pasco recovered himself.

"Nothing. I am stunned. This has turned my head. Lend me your arm. I must go in. No—I must return home—get me another horse—I cannot stay. Quick; I must return—oh, be quick."

"Well, that's coorious!" said the landlord. "I reckon you ought to go in and listen to what the lawyer has to say, first. As for horses, I don't keep 'em, and the lawyer's post-horses be gone into the stable for the night."

"Lend me your arm," said Pepperill. "I don't know right what I'm about. This has come on me quite unexpected."

"I wish three thousand pounds'd come unexpected on me," replied the host.

Pasco entered the room where the lawyer was eating.

"That's right," said the latter. "Take a snack. There's some for all, I say, with my rasher, and you may say so with your legacy, and give me a slice off your dish. Polly—a plate and knife and fork for the gentleman."

Pepperill seated himself. He was as if stupefied. Then he put both elbows on the table, though the movement of his right arm pained him, and began to cry.

"That's what I like," said the lawyer. "Feeling, sentiment. It's what we all ought to do. Amen. When grieving is done, there's a couple of eggs left. But I like that. Heart in the right place. Quite so. What is your tipple? That's very nice. Feeling—I love it. I didn't know, though, that you had seen your uncle for twenty years, and cared twopence about him. P'r'aps you didn't in times gone by; now, of course, it's different with three thousand pounds. I respect your emotion; I love it. But cry when you go to bed. Eat now. There is a place and there is a time for everything. It does you credit, I shall make a point of mentioning it—no extra charge."

END OF VOL. II.

Printed in Great Britain
by Amazon

49551452R00067